Dovi

The Vorge Crew – Book Two

By Laurann Dohner

Dovis by Laurann Dohner

Sold into slavery as a child, Mari was raised on a vessel repair station, growing up to become a highly prized engineer. So she's surprised when her owner not only grants her freedom, but finds her a paying job aboard The Vorge. Mari's determined to impress her new captain and crewmates. It's the only way she'll remain free, safe from the hands of other slavers. But there seems no impressing Dovis, the ship's head of security. He's huge, hairy, scary, and seems to hate humans.

Dovis finds humans weak and annoying at the best of times. They don't need another one aboard The Vorge. Especially a female who works hard enough to make everyone else look lazy. He wants Mari gone—until he meets her. The tiny human is sweet, shy, timid…beautiful. Now Dovis really wants her gone. He isn't happy about his attraction to a human. Especially when he can't be certain Mari's desire for him is from the heart…or an accident of his own making.

The Vorge Crew Series List

Cathian

Dovis

Dovis by Laurann Dohner

Copyright © August 2018

Editor: Kelli Collins

Cover Art: Dar Albert

ISBN: 978-1-944526-95-5

ALL RIGHTS RESERVED. The unauthorized reproduction or distribution of this copyrighted work is illegal, except for the case of brief quotations in reviews and articles.

Criminal copyright infringement is investigated by the FBI and is punishable by up to 5 years in federal prison and a fine of $250,000.

All characters and events in this book are fictitious. Any resemblance to actual persons living or dead is coincidental.

Chapter One	**6**
Chapter Two	**19**
Chapter Three	**39**
Chapter Four	**54**
Chapter Five	**70**
Chapter Six	**85**
Chapter Seven	**97**
Chapter Eight	**111**
Chapter Nine	**129**
Chapter Ten	**141**

Dovis – The Vorge Crew – Book Two

By Laurann Dohner

Chapter One

It was tough being an alien. The fact that Mari was human made it ten times rougher. No one from Earth had made a good impression after they'd taken to space. Many had become thieves or slave traders. She didn't blame most races for their mistrust. Her own family had sold her at the age of ten for money.

What kind of people do that?

Not good ones.

Mari had been one of the luckier kids sold as far as slavery went. She'd been bought by a Teki family that ran a ship repair station. They'd taught her to fix darn near anything that could fly in space. Her small size and quick ability to learn had been assets, earning her respect.

That meant safety from harm, since she was valued. The Teki race viewed humans as disgusting to look upon because they only had two arms and no tentacles. Some of their customers didn't agree, and they frequently tried to touch her. They were painfully discouraged by her owners. The Teki protected Mari with lethal force when necessary.

Freedom wasn't a word she'd dared even whisper. That got slaves killed or punished faster than refusing to do what they were told. And Mari always did as she was told.

That's why dread filled her when K'pa called her into his office after her shift ended. He was the current head of household and ran the station for his family. It never boded well when the alien who held her life in his tentacles wanted a face-to-face meeting.

All six of his eyes stared at her while his two mouths had curved upward in what passed for smiles. "You're done here."

Panic and fear set in right away. She scrambled to think of how she'd messed up. The retrofit of the engine she'd just finished had gone perfectly. She'd even been a day ahead of schedule.

"Please don't push me out an airlock! I'm sorry for whatever I've done. I'll try harder." She was ready to drop to her knees to plead for her life.

He snorted, which passed as laugher for a Teki. "You've made us a lot of money, Mari. I'm finally old enough for a mate and to have children of my own." He leaned forward, four of his tentacles resting on his desk. "P'ski is taking over."

A shudder ran down her spine. He was K'pa's younger brother. Any little mistake caused him to lose his temper. He also thought the workers were treated too nicely and had bragged about making lots of changes when his day to run the repair station came. Some of those changes included longer hours and less meals provided each day. He'd also complained the workers were dressed too nicely for slaves. He'd threatened to make them walk around naked to save credits.

K'pa leaned back in his chair. "You are free, Mari. My gift to you for excellent service and the fortune you helped me make over the years. I've saved well for my family-time retirement. No one is a better mechanic than you." He snorted again. "Plus, it's a matter of honor. With you off the station, repairs will likely fall behind." His double set of lips curved upward again. "P'ski thinks he can do better than I have at running our business. I won't allow that."

Shock held her mute as she stood there, trying to process everything he'd said.

"There is a ship currently in for repairs that has another human onboard. Captain Cathian Vellar is an ambassador for the Tryleskian planet. They abhor slavery and treat other races with respect. I wanted to find you a good home." He used a tentacle to open a drawer and pull out a data card, shoving it her way.

She accepted it and glanced down fast. Her image had been duplicated on the card, some sort of identification.

"I negotiated good wages and living conditions for you upon his ship. He promised to protect you against harm in all ways. I know you sometimes fear others, since we've had issues over the years with customers when they'd spotted you. You're pathetically defenseless, with your lack of claws and your puny size. The captain expects you when you leave my office. Go right to his ship on port three. You are to report directly to him. That card is your pass to freedom."

"Thank you." It was terrifying to leave the familiar for something new, but P'ski scared her more. Working for him would become a nightmare.

"You've never given me any trouble, Mari. Never tried to escape. You were the best slave I ever purchased."

She'd had nowhere to go, and had been smart enough to stay where she'd been protected. Even repair workers heard the whispered rumors of how bad it could be off the station for anyone traveling alone. Slavers might capture them, and they could end up in far worse circumstances. The Teki fed their workers three times a day, gave them access to medical care if they were injured, and issued new clothing every year. They might be locked into their sleeping quarters after a shift, but they had clean, solitary rooms, which kept them safe. No one could molest them, or steal them away.

"Thank you." She bowed her head, clutching the card in her hand.

"I wouldn't have sold you if you'd been *my* spawn," K'pa said. "For a human, you are smart. Your parents were not. I made certain Captain Vellar is aware of your value despite how you look. I vouched for what a hard and dedicated worker you are. He is intelligent and will treat you good. Make me proud again."

The door behind her opened and she spun, heart pounding. It was K'pa's assistant. The alien held a large tool case. "I packed her personal belongings inside, master."

"Escort her to port three, Ri. If anyone asks, she's fixing something. My brother is paranoid I'll pull a stunt of this magnitude—and he's correct." He snorted. "Make certain she gets there without delay. You'll be punished if she doesn't leave on that ship."

"Yes, master." The assistant, a blue-skinned fish-looking alien with three legs, fixed his watery eyes on her. "Let's go, human."

She turned to K'pa again. "I can't thank you enough. Good luck finding a fertile mate, and I hope you have many healthy spawn. I'll never forget you."

She spun before he could change his mind and hurried out the door after the assistant. The tool case must have contained her clothing. She kept close to the blue alien as they left the offices and mingled with the station visitors there for repairs. Many aliens stopped talking as they passed, and she could feel their stares. Mari kept her chin down and her gaze locked on the assistant's back.

They made it to port three without being stopped. Ri led her to one of the docking sleeves and turned, holding out the case.

"This is *The Vorge*. Swipe the card. You've already been hired. It allows you access."

"Thank you." She took the case from him, gripping it with her free hand.

Ri blocked her way to the scanner, and she looked up.

"May I give you words of advice?"

"I would appreciate that."

"Work hard, don't be talkative, and stay out of the way. The best workers are ones who aren't seen but do their jobs efficiently. I've been an assistant for thirty-two years and am considered the best."

"I'll remember." She felt that was good advice.

He stepped out of the way. "Enter."

She scanned the card. The ship doors opened and she rushed inside. They sealed at her back and she stared around, looking for any crew since she didn't know the layout. She hadn't even been able to glimpse what kind of ship it was from the docking sleeve. Port three was for large vessels, though. "Hello? Computer?"

"Activated, Mechanic Mari. What may I help you with?"

The computer already knew her. She smiled. "Please inform Captain Vellar I'm aboard, and I'll wait here until he's ready to see me."

A moment later, lights along the floor activated. "Please follow. I've been instructed to show you to your cabin. The captain is busy at the moment."

"Thank you." She was impressed with the lighting system as she wound her way through a few corridors to a lift. She stepped inside when the doors opened and it took her two levels down. There were six in all— and it was *her* responsibility to keep everything, on every level, in working order. It seemed a bit of a staggering task without a team. Did she have a team? She wasn't sure.

"One step at a time," she whispered.

The doors parted—and she startled when a trio of short, round aliens stood in front of the lift. She'd never seen their kind before but forced a smile. "Hello. I'm the new mechanic. My name is Mari."

"Address us as Pods. It's what we are. To speak to one is to speak to us all. We also should inform you that we read minds. Some aliens find that disturbing. Currently, you are slightly afraid, confused, and worried. There's no reason to be. Captain Vellar is a wonderful boss. We're here to show you to your cabin and answer your questions. The captain and his mate are having sex."

"Again," another one of the Pods muttered.

The third one giggled. "A happy captain means less for us to do."

The first Pod snorted. "That is not correct, or we'd be watching entertainment instead of settling the new mechanic into her cabin."

She bit her lip, prepared to tell them that the computer could do that and they shouldn't bother with her.

"You're crew," the first one stated. "The computer is not. Captain Vellar appreciates a personal touch."

She was immediately reminded the aliens could read minds. That was going to be tough to live with. What if they picked up thoughts she didn't want to share? It was important that the crew like her.

"We won't tell others what you are thinking. That would be considered rude, and we enjoy peace."

"Peace?" She tried to figure out what they meant.

"To anger other crew means we are left without peace. Their thoughts bombard us with their fury," one of them stated. "Any mind that focuses on us send us their thoughts, whether we are scanning for them or not."

"If you are ever in distress, think deeply of us," another one added. "We'll hear you."

The third one bobbed a little. "We don't like to cause anger in our crewmates. Nara still calls Dovis "Wolfman" and "werewolf" in her head. He'd be angry if he knew. We never tell him."

"You just blabbed," the second one accused. "Let One speak. He's best at it."

Mari glanced at them. "You're numbered?"

The one on the far right answered. "I'm One. I'm the voice most of the time because Two has a big mouth and he tends to be grumpy. Three thinks everything is funny and tells bad jokes."

She smiled, liking that they might look similar, but they seemed to have very different personalities.

"She's smart," the middle one grunted. "I like you too, Mari. You're okay for a recently freed slave. We worried that you'd be beaten down and emotionally broken."

"I like that she didn't compare us to Humpty Dumpty," the last one chuckled.

She was confused. "Who or what is that?"

One backed up. "I'm not reading that you are comparing us to childhood memories of storybooks in your mind. You're different from Nara. She's the other human from Earth aboard *The Vorge*, and she is the captain's mate. Come with us, Mari. You should like your cabin. They are far nicer than the ones you had."

"You can see where I lived in my mind?" She was impressed if they could.

"We just read thoughts. We can't see images. You are hoping for a bigger bed and thinking how uncomfortable the narrow cot was in your old quarters. You also had to share a bathroom with two crew teams." One spun away. "Follow us. You have private cabin here. No bathroom sharing required."

They were cute, what with their white rounded bodies, but she worried they'd fall over with those short, tiny legs. They only reached to her waist.

Three chuckled. "She thinks we're cute!"

Crap. Sorry.

"No need to apologize," One sounded amused. "You'll adjust to us, and we like you already."

They led her to a door that auto-opened. Her new quarters *were* nice. She knew her mouth gaped open a little at the generous size. It held furniture to create a living area, with an open bedroom behind. There were doors she could slide together to separate the space. In the very back, there was a storage closet and a private bathroom.

"She likes it," One announced. "It's at least fifteen times the size of her old sleeping room. Do you know how to use the food replicator?"

She walked into the living space and found the device inserted in the wall. "Yes. I've worked on a lot of these updated models."

"She's never eaten from one though," Two stated. "She's wondering if the food quality is better. It is, Mari."

She smiled at them. "Thank you. I have some questions."

"You do not have a team of repair workers. It's just you. Of course, the captain expects you to ask for help if needed. Dovis is the one to contact. He's security, but he has also doubled as our mechanic." One inched closer.

"He's not good at it," Two snorted. "And he gets angry."

"Very." Three laughed. "We've learned many bad words from him."

One sighed. "She wants to explore her cabin and learn the ship. The computer will give you schematics of the vessel and a list of repairs that need to be done. I believe all the parts have been ordered. Most are minor repairs that Dovis refused to do. You can start tomorrow at six."

"Thank you." Mari already felt excited to start.

The trio left her alone and the doors sealed. She stared in wonder at her nice living quarters, grinning. She was free—and now she had a new crew, which she hoped she'd like. "Computer, can you show me a detailed design of the ship?"

The wall lit up and she walked closer. It was her job to get to know every inch of the large vessel and keep it functioning. *The Vorge* was her new home—and Mari enjoyed a good challenge.

* * * * *

Dovis snarled, punching the bag. The computer had just notified him that the new crew member had boarded. He probably should meet with the human, but he had no desire to do so. Cathian had completely disregarded his wishes.

He wondered if this Mari would be as annoying as Nara. She always made jokes about fetching a ball around him. He understood that on Earth they had dogs. He'd even done his research, finding a hologram of what one looked like, and understood the comparison. It was still an insult.

He pounded the bag harder with his fists.

York entered the training room and gave him a nod. "Did you hear? The new mechanic has arrived."

"I was informed."

"Think she'd wanna do a Parri?"

He gazed at his friend. "Nara says you look like the love child of a blue vampire and the industrial Hulk. What do *you* think? Did you research them?"

York growled, revealing his teeth, including the two extended fangs. "Incredible. Not industrial. It is a large creature. I'll assume she compared me to a blue vampire because of my coloring and tearing fangs."

"That's Nara. She thinks she's funny."

His friend approached. "Cathian mated her. It means humans are sexually compatible. I can't disregard that. You saw the brothel workers on the last four stations we've visited. I want to get laid."

"What about Marrow? You were having sex with her."

York sighed, shoulders sagging. "She is set on finding a mate, now that the captain's got one. I'm not the one for her. She is envious of how happy those two are. She discovered Nara hadn't had sex in over a year, and thinks that's what might have landed her Cathian. It convinced her to go celibate."

"Cathian was in heat and the crew threw Nara into his cabin. I doubt he cared how long it had been since another male had touched her, and *she* had no choice."

"Tell that to Marrow. I tried but she is convinced otherwise. She won't touch me and hasn't since Cathian mated. I miss sex so much, it's depressing."

"The Teki women didn't do it for you on this station?" Dovis grinned.

"I could get past the tentacles but the two mouths freaked me out. Which one are you supposed to kiss?"

"You kiss brothel workers?" Dovis snorted a laugh. "Brave."

"I can't get hard without kissing."

"I didn't know that about the Parri."

"At least we don't go into heat. That's a plus. The Yang have razor-sharp teeth, so that station was out. I wanted to keep my tongue. Hermios only fuck underwater, and I'd drown. The Bing disturbed me. I refuse to engage in a fist fight and have to violently pin down a woman just to get her in the mood. Not to mention, they bite and use their claws because it's hotter for them if males are bleeding. The Glaxion women looked at me like a test subject they wanted to study. It made me too nervous to consider getting naked with one. I haven't gotten laid since Marrow visited my cabin before the captain went into heat. What about you?"

"I did a Bing."

His friend's mouth dropped open, his eyes wide.

Dovis shrugged. "I enjoy an aggressive romp. And as for the biting part, I just bend them over to keep their mouths away from me."

"We were at that station months ago."

"I'm aware."

"Do you go into heat?"

"Not like Cathian. I handle it myself. I don't need a female to get me through it."

York grinned. "Are you that flexible? Impressive."

"Fuck you." Dovis laughed though. "I use my hands. A few days of jacking off does the trick, and I'm not forced to be stuck with a female forever. It's a reasonable solution."

"What do you mean, stuck forever?"

"My kind permanently bond to a female while in heat. It's a done deal if my sperm enters one. I keep my dick far from females during that time."

"*Damn.*"

"It is what it is."

"I hope this mechanic is hot and tall. Large breasts would be nice. I like Nara but she's too small for me. She swears a lot of humans are bigger than her. I want one of those, but they're very rare out in space. I can't believe Cathian even found one." York smiled. "And I hope she likes the color blue."

"The captain didn't find her. She was found for him. Anyway, good luck with that."

"You're not going to compete with me if she's attractive?"

"Hell no. Humans are brash, outspoken, and annoying. I'll pass. She's yours if you want to stick your dick in her."

"Crude."

"I'm just being honest."

The computer dinged.

Dovis walked over to the wall. "What is it?"

"Captain Cathian wishes to depart. You are to report to the bridge."

"Tell him I'll be there in five. I need to take a fast shower."

"Transferring the message," the computer replied.

Dovis spun, heading to the doors. "See you later."

"Why does he always make you go to the bridge?"

"In case of attack. Sometimes ships try to follow us. I get to blow shit up in that event. No way am I missing that."

York chuckled. "I call dibs on the human then."

"Have at it—and good luck."

Chapter Two

Mari wiggled her hips and reached in front of her, dug her fingers into the crevice, and used her bare toes to push forward. Layers of dirt covered her baggy clothes, the material she wore acting like a dust cloth. It was cramped in the air vent but she just fit.

An intake grate came up on her left. She twisted to her side and reached for the can attached to the side of her pant leg. The spray foamed over the metal, eating at the dirty gunk that had accumulated.

Once she finished cleaning all the vents, the air quality on the ship would improve. It would smell better too. This was one of the chores Dovis had probably refused to do since, according to the maintenance logs, the cleaning schedule had lapsed for a few months.

She watched as the foam melted, revealing gleaming metal minus the gunk. Only a hundred and twenty-three more to go. She clipped the can back onto her leg, flattened to her belly, and crawled forward.

A quick glance at her watch told her she had four more hours before her first official shift started on her new job. Nervous energy had kept her from sleeping. It might impress her new boss that she'd used her free time to clean, or it might piss him off. She was willing to risk it.

She made it to the next intake grate and sprayed it down. Once the foam cleared, she stared out into an empty hallway on the second deck. No one seemed to be up yet. The Pods were the only crew she'd seen on the ship so far.

Mari used her toes to push forward as she wiggled down the vent. The auto light strapped to her head turned on when the next section had no grates to allow her any illumination.

Maybe Dovis wasn't a small alien and couldn't perform the task. Even the Pods would have been hard-pressed to fit. They might be short but they were pretty round. She squirmed some more, grabbed wall seams, and pulled forward until her auto light clicked off when another grate appeared ahead.

The vent widened a bit, and the grate was larger than the rest. She was able to rise to her knees and crawl toward it. Not as much gunk layered the metal bars. She inched closer to peer out into what appeared to be a crew gym. Weights and exercise machines were set up, along with a big area with padding. She sat on her butt, removed the can, and sprayed.

Just as she attached the can to her thigh, a noisy hiss sounded.

Mari froze.

"Fuck," a deep male voice snarled, the sound followed by a loud boom.

The foam melted and Mari instantly wiggled backward away from the large grate. An alien had entered the gym. He was tall, wide chested, and very furry. Two pointed ears stuck up from the sides of his head near the top. His mouth and nose were pushed outward, forming a small muzzle. Sharp teeth flashed as he snarled again and stormed toward the weights in the far corner.

He reminded her of an alien she'd once seen during a repair. Another big furry beast with sharp teeth. The doors to a vessel had opened and a small, hairless animal had rushed out on four legs. The much larger beast had captured it. She'd watched, horrified, as it ate the much smaller one in a few large bites of blood and gore.

Fear swamped her. Was one of the crew members an alien eater? Would he view her as food?

Her gaze lowered to his big hands. They were covered in fur on the back and as he gripped a weighted bar, she spotted thick, sharp claws. A chill ran down her spine and Mari inched deeper into the vent, not wanting to draw his attention. He looked tall enough to reach the grate near the ceiling and just rip her out.

More snarls tore from him as he pumped the weights up and down in his arms. His back was massive and as furry as his front, a light brown shade. He wore pants and boots but no shirt. His form was like a human male—if humans were born with fur. He possessed two legs and arms, but she didn't spot a tail. The other beast she'd seen had one, and it hadn't worn pants, either.

She was afraid to move. The vents tended to creak from her weight as she crawled in them. What if he heard her and attacked? She didn't want to become like that hairless animal, and find herself devoured. Of course, she was bigger. It would probably take him thirty or so bites to eat her for a meal.

Another shudder ran down her spine, along with more fear at those horrible thoughts. Had she been sold to a ship with a dangerous crew?

The door to the gym opened again and a human woman walked in. "Do you ever sleep, Dovis?"

The big beast of a male snarled.

"Who pissed you off this early in the morning cycle?"

He turned, his dark eyes gleaming with scary intent. Mari tensed, hoping she wasn't about to see the human get eaten. He dropped the heavy weight bar with a crash. "Shouldn't you still be with your life-lock?"

"Probably." The human laughed. "Cathian does like to keep me in bed. Then again, he had some ambassador gig to attend to on the comms system and, time changes being what they are, it was in the middle of our sleep cycle. So what's *your* problem?"

"We don't need another crew member."

The human nodded and put her hands on her hips. "Ah. Is it because she's my race, or is it just because it's another body you aren't permitted to beat on?"

He stormed closer but stopped before invading her personal space, towering a good foot or so over the human. He was way bigger, with his broad arms and chest. "Both. Cathian hired a recently freed slave. It's a security risk. We know nothing about this human. The chances of her being resentful are great. I believe Cathian made a mistake hiring her. Even you have admitted most humans are not people you trust. He won't listen to me. We were doing fine without her."

"You're being paranoid. Humans aren't all bad. It's bullshit to say we were doing fine. Should I mention the clog in my bath drain because you ignored my request to fix it? My life-lock sheds from his mane. I miss my hot soaks, damn it. The food replicator on the bridge only makes drinks. You were supposed to fix or replace it. It's been that way for two months. Everyone is tired of starving while on shift when they forget to bring snacks. No one else is sorry that Cathian finally hired someone who will do the stuff you won't. It's all on *you*, Dovis. No one else."

He growled, looking further annoyed.

Mari waited for the big furry beast to attack the woman who seemed to either be foolish or insane to purposely engage in an argument with him. It didn't happen, though. The beast backed off.

"I would have attended to those repairs, Nara."

"In what year, Dovis? This one? Next? We needed help and now we have it." The human suddenly stepped closer and waggled a finger at him. "Don't forget what Cathian told you. No more trying to scare the crew to make them quit. You don't like people. Understood. That doesn't mean you can be a grump to everyone. We've already lost our last maintenance engineer because of your crappy ability to get along with others. Harver quit because of *you*." She dropped her hand to her side. "I'm going to personally assure the woman that you aren't allowed to hurt her. I'll give her a shock collar for your throat and a remote if you pull your usual shit. I bet *that* would make her feel safer if you decide to be an asshole. I don't care if that means you receive a dozen shocks a day. She stays!"

He snarled again.

The human spun, marching toward the doors. "I mean it."

Dovis turned and punched a dent into the wall. He threw back his head next and his muzzle parted, letting loose a terrifying howl of rage. It seemed he didn't like to be threatened. Mari flinched, covering her ears. He stormed out of the gym. She breathed easier once he was gone and crawled back into the tighter part of the vent to continue her job.

That guy was going to make her life difficult. She just knew it. Would she really push the button if the human put a shock collar on him? The Teki used them sometimes on new slaves they'd purchased who refused to take orders. She'd witnessed their punishment, dropping to the ground and suffering what appeared to be seizures while being shocked. It looked extremely unpleasant and painful. She felt sick just thinking about being responsible for doing that to someone else.

"Nope. Never," she muttered. "Unless he tries to eat me. Then…probably."

She sprayed the next grate and crawled on. Her priority list changed. She needed to go fix that tub drain. The repair had only listed a cabin number, not who the cabin belonged to.

She hurried through the vents. By the time her work shift started, she estimated she'd be finished cleaning one entire level.

That should impress her new boss. She'd completed a task before being officially on the work clock. An excellent employee was one a boss would want to keep around. As good as K'pa had been to her, that didn't mean another owner would treat her well if the captain decided to fire her.

"Never again," she whispered, spraying another vent. "I'm keeping my freedom."

She reached a sharp turn and had to wiggle a lot to make it. The schematics of the ship said there was a lone crew cabin in this direction but she didn't know who it belonged to. It was odd, because all the other crew cabins were grouped together on another levels. She just hoped whoever it belonged to wouldn't be home while she cleaned the final two grates.

Mari saw a light ahead and paused, listening. It was all quiet. She inched forward and peeked through the grate.

The private cabin was larger than her old room by at least four times. No wonder the crew member wanted it. There was a full kitchen built into a corner. The bed was massive and could easily sleep five humans side by side. A long, wide couch sat near an entertainment screen. It was black, stuffed like a puffy cloud, and looked extremely comfortable. She felt a little envious.

Mari noticed horizontal bars up near the ceiling, hanging a few feet down. That made her frown. Was the alien who lived there some kind of bird species? She'd once fixed a ship carrying winged aliens. They liked to hang from perches on the ceiling by their clawed toes while sleeping. But this cabin had a bed, too. Maybe it was a circulation thing for whoever owned the room, and he or she needed to spend some time upside down.

She shrugged and sprayed the vent. The grate was clogged bad enough that she had to respray.

A loud whoosh sounded from the cabin, and she stilled. Had the resident returned?

The foam melted—and she stared in shock at the scary furred beast from the gym. The whoosh had been the shower unit opening to let him out.

Mari couldn't help but stare. Dovis wasn't wearing pants or boots this time. Just a towel wrapped around his furry hips. He shook his body, despite looking mostly dry. The shower unit would have dried him, except sometimes if you had a lot of hair, it would remain damp. She figured he had that problem all over his body instead of just the top of his head, the way most species did.

He stretched his arms up, twisted his head a little, and then walked toward a clothing storage cabinet near the shower.

She was too afraid to crawl away or make a noise. He'd probably be pissed to find her inside his vent. It was clear he resented her being hired.

He yanked open the storage door and she squeezed her eyes closed when he lowered his hand to tear off the towel. Curiosity had her peeking though, wanting to know if he actually did have a tail.

His legs were human in shape, and he had a super muscular ass covered in brown fur. She had her answer. No tail.

He tossed the discarded towel in the laundry shoot and stretched again, this time twisting his upper body a little. The garment he withdrew from the closet was like a blue, thin, stretchy wrap that he tied around his hips. He faced her, and she held her breath as he crossed the large cabin, getting closer.

Mari pushed back against the vent wall as much as possible. What if he saw her? Heard her? The hum from the engines should hide her soft breathing sounds but he had those big pointed ears. It implied he might have hypersensitive hearing.

He walked over to the fluffy black cloud of a couch and threw himself at it, twisting in the air and landing on his back. He reached over, grabbed the controller for the entertainment screen, and flipped it on. Strange music filled the room. It wasn't unpleasant or loud, but a slow, appealing beat.

Mari knew it was time to go. The noises would mask any creaking the vent made.

She crawled forward and came upon the second grate. It hurt her work ethic to leave it be, but no way could she risk cleaning it with him in his room. He might see the fresh foam if he happened to look toward that wall before it melted.

She glanced out as she inched past the grate. He remained on the couch...but something about him looked different. Her mouth fell open as it clicked that his fur seemed shorter.

It wasn't her imagination. As she kept watching, his fur seemed to be shrinking away. Within a minute, Dovis was no longer covered in fur, but firm light brown skin.

Mari knew her mouth was still hanging open.

He rolled to his side, giving her a view of his face. She almost gasped, and quickly clamped a hand over her mouth to avoid making a sound. His bones had changed too. He didn't look exactly human, but even closer than he already had. His muzzle had pushed inward to leave a nose instead of snout. His previously thin lips were fuller now that they weren't stretched over a row of sharp teeth. She couldn't help but stare, transfixed. He no longer looked like a beast.

His eyes were closed and, as minutes passed, a low snore came over the soft music. Mari released her mouth and very carefully crawled away. She made it to the intake grate near the lift, cleaned it, and then opened it to drop into the corridor. It was tough to reach that high to close it again. She had to jump a few times, but her fingers managed to push it closed enough to auto-engage the lock.

She'd heard about shapeshifting aliens, of course. Slaves loved to gossip about the ships they'd worked on and the strange crew members they'd seen. One of her fellow slaves, Bargnor, had shared a story of meeting a tall species that could shrink in size. They went from nine feet tall with slim bodies to three feet of solid, bulky mass. He'd been told it was some kind of social requirement for them to walk around in their tall forms, but while they worked, their smaller, bulkier bodies were needed because they were stronger that way.

Dovis seemed the opposite. His social form was scary as hell, with his fur and that muzzle full of teeth. But his sleeping form must revert to skin. It was strange, but then again, most aliens were to Mari. She shrugged it off as she got into the lift, returning to her room to shower and change into clean clothes in case the captain wanted to finally meet her. Good impressions could mean life or death.

* * * * *

Dovis seethed as he entered the dining room. He'd awoken to reports about the new crew member. Mari from Earth had worked tirelessly while he'd slept the day shift away. Not only had she replaced the food replicator on the bridge, but she'd unclogged the tub in Cathian's cabin. Nara had personally sent him a message to rub it in.

It pissed him off. The human was trying to make him look bad.

York waved him to his table. He nodded, stopped at the counter to get his breakfast that Midgel had cooked, and took a seat across from his friend.

"How was your day shift?"

York grumbled over his dinner meal.

"Was Cathian on a tear about something? Were there problems?"

"No. I met Mari."

Dovis felt hopeful. "Is she horrible? Rude? Disrespectful? Is Cathian ready to drop her at the next station?"

"No." York sighed and met his gaze. "She's actually very timid and super polite. It's her damn size."

"I don't understand."

"She's smaller than Nara. Not too much in height, but she's thin. I'd break her if I attempted to have sex with her." York grumbled again. "I'm disappointed. I guess I should have remembered she was a slave. Their masters probably don't feed them much, right?" His mood suddenly brightened. "That's it! I'll get her to eat, so she gains lots of weight and gets some padding over those dainty bones of hers. That would cushion her some."

Dovis bit back a snarl and shoved a piece of meat into his mouth.

York grinned now. "She's attractive. Her hair is super long. I don't think they allowed her to cut it as a slave. She keeps it in three braids that are mingled together down her back, but it reaches her little butt, maybe a bit longer. She's a great worker, too. She completed twice as many tasks in an hour as Harver did when he was still in charge of maintenance. It surprised me. She's such a little thing. You'd think she'd get tired easily. Nara had to track her down to make her stop to eat lunch. The little human maybe didn't know she's allowed meal breaks. Poor thing. I can't imagine being a slave."

Dovis felt his chest vibrate from a low growl. He didn't want another human onboard. Nara was more than enough.

"What's your problem?"

"She is trying to make me look bad."

York laughed.

"It's not amusing."

York nodded and ate his dinner meal. "I think you're being oversensitive and looking for a reason to not like the human. You tend to be suspicious of others you aren't close to. You did beat the shit out of Harver a few dozen times. He feared for his life."

"He invaded my cabin without permission. He deserved to be beaten."

"He was fixing your shower when you beat him last. It wasn't as if he went into your cabin to go through your personal belongings."

"It's *my* space. No one enters. I didn't ask him to fix it. I would have done it myself."

"The computer told him it needed repaired. I know you like your privacy but you did damn near kill him. *That's* why Cathian made you take over his duties once Harver fled. But it was supposed to be a short-term punishment for you running off the guy who kept shit going. Instead, you refused to hire someone else. Cathian finally took matters into his own hands."

"He didn't allow me to run a security check on this Earth woman."

York snorted. "What's the risk? She's human. The scans confirmed it. One hundred percent. Nothing in her body is a danger to the other crew or the ship. No venom glands, no poisons she can secrete…"

"She could be a terrorist who hates Tryleskians. Maybe she wants to blow up *The Vorge*. She has the skills."

York laughed again.

"I'm not joking. We know nothing about her."

"I do. I read the recommendation letter from her previous owner."

Dovis stopped eating. "What recommendation? Cathian didn't tell me he had any kind of paperwork on her."

"Probably because you'd try to use it against her." York took a sip of his drink. "She was sold at the age of ten by her parents." Anger flashed in his eyes. "Someone would have to kill me to take my offspring. I'd fight to the death to defend them. I did research on humans when Cathian took Nara for his mate. Our captain is protective of her, so I didn't want to accidently offend her in some way. Ten is an age when humans still need guidance and protection from their parents. They are weak and vulnerable. Poor thing was sold instead and left to fend for herself."

"Maybe they sold her because she's a terrorist."

York shook his head. "You sound paranoid—and you're trying to pick a fight."

"You like to fight with me."

"*You* like fighting and making me angry enough to enjoy hitting you. There's a difference. I know you're like this because you want to keep everyone safe. You really take your job seriously. It's your nature to protect the ones you care about. You'll learn that Mari isn't a threat. I also know that will take time. Just don't taunt the human about her bad parents. That would be cruel."

Dovis scowled. "I wouldn't do that."

"You're not allowed to hit her. You'd kill her with one swipe of your claws. Humans are vulnerable basically anywhere on their bodies. Don't forget that. Their skin is fragile and easy to penetrate with sharp objects. They bleed, too."

"I don't hit females."

York snorted. "Wrong. You punched Marrow."

"In her arm…over a year ago. She tried to engage me sexually regardless of my insistence that I would never bed her. I warned her that if she grabbed my dick one more time, I'd hit her."

"I liked it when she grabbed my shaft." York glared at him. "She just wanted to test you out to see if you could be her mate."

"I didn't want her."

"Casual sex is great. What do you have against it?" York paused and his eyebrows rose. "Are you into males?"

"No. My race just has a difficult time getting aroused when we can smell another male on a female. Marrow always smelled like she had done *you* recently."

"That's sad. I didn't know that about your kind. Does that mean you have to find only virgins to screw? Wait—you said you did a Bing. Was she a virgin? Was it her first day on the job at the brothel?"

"I prepared myself."

York's eyebrows rose again as he stared at him.

"I used a drug that dulled my sense of smell to have sex with the Bing. It meant not smelling a damn thing for two full days before it returned. Do you see why I preferred to refuse Marrow? The drug also effects my sense of taste. I like to enjoy my meals. Sex with her wasn't worth it to me. Also, I mentally knew her scent too well. My mind would have known with certainty that she smelled like you. It's a mood killer."

"You poor bastard."

Dovis shoved another piece of meat into his mouth and chewed. "Forget I told you."

"Your race is very secretive. I tried to do research on your planet but not much is out there. Hell, most of you don't even travel in space. Why did you leave Amarai?"

Dovis finished and stood. "That's never a discussion we'll have."

"You wanted a security check done on Mari to find out about her past. Think about that. What are you hiding in yours, my friend?"

Dovis carried his plate to the cleaner and dumped it inside, stomping out of the room. He had a meeting with Cathian. He made it to his friend's office with minutes to spare and entered.

Cathian held up a finger and spoke into a comm unit. "Understood, Rex. I know this trade agreement is important to Tryleskian. I'll take care of it. We've already changed course. My ship will be there in a week."

Dovis took a seat, waiting.

His friend ended the comms and sighed. "Why did I agree to be an ambassador again?"

Dovis's memory flashed to the Nito station, where they'd met years before, and his mood improved. He'd been working as a security guard at the time and the newly appointed ambassador had come to celebrate his position. Cathian had insisted he have a few drinks with him, and their friendship had been instant.

"To avoid being forced to life-lock and breed children with a coldhearted female you detested. Your father put pressure on you to either do so, or represent your people. You chose this."

Cathian chuckled. "It was a rhetorical question. I never regret my decision. Nara makes me happier than I've ever been. I would have been miserable on my home planet. It's just that some duties they ask of me make me want to tear out my mane." He reached up and pointed to his hair. "I'd look silly with bald spots. Today is one of those times."

"What did Rex want?"

"Pets." Cathian lowered both of his hands to his desk and clasped them together.

Dovis gawked at him.

"That's my reaction, too. It seems a male and his life-lock visited Callon planet on vacation and bought a few creatures for their children. They were a hit, and now many families want them. We're going to the planet to negotiate buying enough to breed our own supply."

"What kind of creature is it?"

"I don't know. Rex sent me a vid and the information. I'll go over it later. I was assured one would fit in the palm of my hand and they're sturdy enough to survive inside our cargo hold for weeks. It also means we'll have to set a feeding schedule once we have them. I'm supposed to buy at least a hundred males and females each that aren't related by blood to make good breeding stock."

"I can't believe we're going to be hauling pets." Dovis curled his lip in disgust.

Cathian nodded. "The indignity. I agree. This is the job though. I guess it's better than some duties they've asked of us. We're not going in to negotiate in order to avoid a war. That's something."

"I'd rather fight than babysit creatures."

"I just hope Nara doesn't want one, whatever the hell it is."

Dovis frowned, not liking the idea of some tiny creature running free around *The Vorge*.

Cathian had the nerve to grin. "I knew you'd have that reaction." His features changed into a stern one. "Speaking of, don't try to get rid of the female I just hired. Mari is the best maintenance engineer we've ever had. Not only is she overqualified to keep all machines on this ship working, but she has experience with life support rehauls. The Teki I got her from showed me an invoice for all the work she's done just in the past two years. It deeply impressed me. She's an actual *mechanic* instead of a tinkerer."

"The slave owner would lie to increase the price. How much did you buy her for?"

"I didn't."

That surprised Dovis. "What do you mean?"

"She was granted freedom. He only requested I give her fair treatment, good pay, and protection from harm. Not one credit was exchanged. The Teki seemed very fond of Mari."

"Was she his lover?"

Cathian shook his head. "Teki males aren't sexually compatible with humans."

"Perhaps they found a way."

His friend leaned forward. "Part of my job is to study different alien races, Dovis. The Teki are ones we deal with often. Let me tell you how their males have sex. You've seen them, correct?"

Dovis nodded.

"The male has to lock his tentacles with the female's, attaching their suckers together. They drain fluids from the female that arouse the male, and that makes their shaft fill and swell. It's about the size of your thigh, by the way, when it's ready to be inserted into the female's body—which is now deflated from her fluid loss. A human doesn't make the kind of fluid needed to make his shaft swell. They view humans as visually disgusting. They weren't lovers, Dovis. The Teki kept apologizing to me for Mari being so ugly, but he insisted I could get over her horrid looks once I came to appreciate her skills to repair anything."

"Did he know at the time that your mate is human?"

"No, but I informed him. He'd just heard we had a human aboard and hoped that I might treat Mari well, since we 'hadn't killed or sold ours.'"

"What did he say then?"

"He worried that the crew might sexually assault her. It seems some of the customers have attempted it in the past with his human workers. I assured him that would never happen. None of my crew would force a woman."

"I don't like having another human here. They're not suited for manual labor. The females are even less so."

Cathian unclasped his hands, touched the pad to his right, and handed it over. "Look at day one."

Dovis accepted it and read the checklist of repairs that needed to be done—and all the ones she'd completed so far. He scowled.

His friend's chuckle annoyed him more. "That's more than you did in all the months combined that we were without Harver. Suck it up, Dovis. She stays. Avoid her if you must but I'm with Nara. I'll personally wrestle you down and put a shock collar around your throat if it means Mari feels secure enough that you can't do her any harm. I'd hate to watch you hit the floor twitching in pain, but then again…I'm taking a bath with Nara tonight. Mari fixed the tub drain."

Dovis threw the pad on the desk. "You'd threaten me with a shock collar? I don't hit females. You should know that. You're supposed to be my best friend."

"I am. That's why I'm not going to toss you out an airlock or fire you if you scare Mari. She's timid and frightens easily. Don't use that to intimidate her. You will always be my best friend and head of security, but don't think I won't even out the odds if you pull your normal shit. No aggression displays near her. She stays. Even if that means giving her a way to drop your ass every time you snarl at her."

He wanted to punch something. Mainly, Cathian's amused face. "Anything else?"

"Be nice when you see her. It won't kill you. She's shy. I know Nara likes to engage you in arguments but Mari is very different. She was a slave. I had to order her to meet my gaze and to speak. She's even more timid that Midgel. Keep that in mind. Don't yell at her. She'd probably cry or something. Nobody wants that."

"Cry?" He was alarmed at the thought.

"Humans do that when they are highly fearful or upset."

"Fuck. Midgel doesn't do that, and I've growled at her before when she cooked a meal I didn't like. This Mari sounds pathetic, Cathian."

Cathian rose to his feet fast and snarled. "Are you insulting the race of my mate again?"

"Nara doesn't cry."

"She does, but not from *your* shit. You just piss off my life-lock. Mari isn't like Nara. Do we need to take this to the mats?"

It was tempting. He did love to fight.

Cathian sank back into his chair. "On second thought, forget it. I'm taking that bath with Nara. Not bleeding. Dismissed. Go spar with York if you need to get rid of your aggression. Better yet, pick Raff."

Dovis glared at Cathian, shaking his head.

Cathian chuckled. "No to Raff? Not surprising."

"I know what he used to do. I'm never taking him on." He got up from his chair and left, not wanting to think about the Tryleskian assassin onboard. That was one male he avoided confrontations with at all costs.

Chapter Three

Mari removed her jacket and tossed it onto the floor where she knelt. Sweat coated her skin from the heat of the steam that escaped the panel on the floor, making her fingers slip on the tool. She had to wipe her hands on her pants before attempting it again. The seals began to loosen, and she grinned as the last one released the metal plate. From there, it was easy to spot the problem where the steam leak occurred and assess the damage it had caused to the wiring.

"Got you." She turned to the toolbox resting next to her and opened one of the thin drawers.

"What the hell?"

The deep snarl almost made her scream. Her heart pounded as she twisted her head, staring at Dovis. He wore a black uniform this time that covered not only his legs, but also his chest and arms. Only his clawed hands and scary face showed.

He stepped closer. "What are you doing down here in the middle of a sleep cycle?"

He frightened her enough that she had a difficult time forming words.

He crouched, leaving close, his black eyes gleaming. "Answer. What are you doing?"

"Um, York sent me a message that his steamer in his shower wasn't as hot as it used to be. I went over the system and figured the problem had to be where the unit goes to his cabin, since no one else had filed a repair request," she said, voice barely above a whisper. She dropped her gaze to his covered chest. His eyes freaked her out. They were black and cold-looking. "I was right. Look if you'd like. Some of the wires frayed where the steam was leaking, since it's humid and hot. I planned to replace the wires and fix the broken joint. It's shorting out but not enough to completely shut down the power to his unit."

"It's in the middle of your sleep cycle."

She bit her lip, feeling nervous. "I didn't mean to break a rule, if that's one of them. I'm very sorry." She bowed her head and curled into her chest a bit. "Please forgive me."

"What the hell? Don't do that," he growled.

Now he sounded upset rather than angry. She risked lifting her head just enough to peek at him. He had shrunk back onto his haunches and his black eyes weren't glaring anymore. They appeared wide and startled.

"Please don't punish me. I didn't know I wasn't allowed to work during a sleep cycle. I just wanted York to be able to use his steam when he wakes for his shift. It's important that everyone like me so I can stay."

"Fuck." He shot to his feet and backed far away from her. "Who said anything about punishment? I'm not going to hit you. I was just surprised to find you here while I did my rounds. I expected you to be asleep along with the rest of the crew."

She almost relaxed. "I didn't break a rule?"

"No. It's just weird. You should be sleeping, too."

"This was more important." She calmed. No rules had been broken, and that meant no punishment. "I'll be done in about fifteen minutes."

He muttered something under his breath that she couldn't hear. Then he turned away and left her alone again. She returned to the task. The gloves she dug out of the toolbox were a bit big but they worked fine to protect her skin from getting a shock as she replaced the wires and cracked joint. Now the system should work perfectly without any problems.

She put the plate back over the deck flooring and sealed it tight. It only took her a moment to clean up her mess, return the gloves to her toolbox, close it, and toss the jacket over her arm. She left to go to the lift that would take her to her cabin.

The sight of Dovis waiting by the lift had her steps slowing. He turned, maybe sensing or hearing her approach. She came to a halt.

"I didn't mean to scare you." His voice was deep still but he was no longer snarling. "That thing you said, about people liking you...well, that's bullshit. Cathian and Nara are determined to keep you. Sleep next time and allow a repair to wait. York wouldn't want you missing sleep to give him more steam." He grumbled something else under his breath.

"What?"

"Nothing."

He came toward her suddenly, and her entire body went rigid. He didn't strike her though, but instead tore the toolbox from her fingers. He backed away with it.

"It looks heavy, and you're too thin. There's no rule that says you must limit what you eat. As much as you care to consume is a crew benefit that comes with the job. Why do you have Harver's jacket?"

"I didn't steal it." She stared at the floor. "The Pods said I could have anything in the maintenance locker that was left behind from the person who had this job before me. I'll put it back."

He frowned. "I didn't accuse you of anything. Stop assuming the worst. I was curious why you have it, that's all."

"I needed to crawl into the Y shaft first to see if the steam problem started there. It's very cold since it's next to the outer hull of the ship. I was freezing, and then I remembered seeing the jacket. Once I realized the problem had to be a direct link to York's cabin, I just didn't return the jacket to the locker."

"You shouldn't wear something that baggy. It could get caught while you're working around moving parts."

"I'm aware, but that wasn't the case tonight. I knew it had to be a connection problem once I inspected the Y shaft."

"Next time, wear your own jacket."

She opened her mouth but then closed it. *Never fight or talk back to a superior.* It was an important rule to remember.

"Is that a problem?"

She swallowed. "I don't have a jacket, master. I only own four outfits. The Teki sent me with a tool case but it had been stripped of my work gear. No gloves, jacket, safety boots, or chemical suit. Luckily, the last worker here left his behind."

He snarled. She jumped.

"Stop reacting that way," he said. "You're too sensitive to sounds. You should have informed Cathian or me of your lack of clothing. It's

43

dangerous if the uniforms you're required to wear are ill-fitting. Why didn't you speak up?"

"I don't want to be a nuisance."

"Hauling your ass to med bay to have you patched up or explaining why you died to the captain would be a nuisance. I'll send a message to the Pods to correct this mess. It's not as if they have much else to do. They can have proper equipment replicated to fit you, including uniforms and other outfits. You can't live in four sets of clothing. I'll return this toolbox to the maintenance locker. Give me the jacket."

She passed it over, careful to avoid his sharp-looking claws. "Thank you, master."

"Call me Dovis. I'm not your owner. I'm head of security, and the one you should come to if the captain is busy. Next time, speak up if there's something you need. Your job is secure. Nara saw to that."

He spun away, called for the lift, and got in when it opened.

She didn't move.

"Are you getting in?"

"I'll wait. You're going down. My cabin is up two floors."

"Fine. Go to bed. That's an order. You need sleep. Accidents happen if you're too tired to focus on your duties."

The lift doors closed and she breathed easier. "At least he didn't try to eat me."

Dovis ignored the low vibrations coming from his chest. It happened when he was upset.

The female wasn't anything like he'd expected. She had large dark brown eyes that he'd enjoyed staring into. Her features were strangely appealing too. That had stunned him since Nara wasn't attractive to him. He was certain he'd feel that way about all human females. That wasn't true. Mari had tempted him to reach out to see if her skin felt as soft as it looked. It left him unsettled.

He was also angry with *himself*. The sweet scent of her fear made him feel guilty. It wasn't something that had ever happened before. He normally liked that reaction from anyone he met.

York had been correct. Mari appeared too thin. It was possible malnutrition had also stunted her growth. He remembered she'd been a child when sold into slavery. She was shorter than Nara by a good inch. Of course, York had probably been paying more attention to her breasts than her height.

It bothered him that she hadn't felt the need to tell any of the crew that her previous owner had sent her with so few possessions. Her loose clothing could put her in danger.

He contacted the Pods. One of them answered, sounding disorientated and sleepy.

"It's rude to wake us. What do you want, Dovis? It better be urgent."

It sounded like the ill-tempered one. "Two, first thing in the morning, replicate Mari some clothing and everything she'll need to do her job. Those bastards on the repair station sent her with next to nothing. That includes a coat, gloves and fire suit. Understand?"

"This couldn't have waited?"

"No," he said, ending the call.

He returned the toolbox and jacket to the maintenance locker before heading to the bridge. He took a seat in the captain's chair and stared out at dark space, finally relaxing.

He liked being alone...most of the time. Dovis was good at it. He'd been sentenced to outcast status the moment his mother had birthed him on Amarai and had fled the planet the first chance he'd gotten at the age of fifteen.

Past memories of his childhood surfaced but he pushed them back. They only made him angry.

A red light flashed on the console before him, and he straightened just as the computer announced a problem. He hopped out of the seat and approached the pilot controls, his fingers flying over the screen to get more information.

Suddenly, there was some kind of power surge—and the engines shut down.

An alarm blared.

He silenced it fast, scanning all the readouts. Power seemed stable all over the ship except to the engines. They refused to restart or respond. Next, he checked if any other ships were in range. Nothing showed on the radar.

He turned, opening comms. "Cathian? We have a problem."

Long seconds passed before his friend's voice responded. "What?"

"The engines went down and aren't restarting. We're floating dead in space but internal power and life support haven't been effected."

"Did we hit something? Are we under attack?"

"I don't think so. I'm leaving the bridge to go down to the engines to see what the hell happened. The computer isn't reading the problem. It only registered some kind of power surge before the engines shut down. I just wanted to let you know what's going on."

"Call Mari to help."

"I've got this."

"Damn your stubborn ass! She's our mechanic. Wake her, Dovis. That's an order."

He snarled, ending comms and storming off the bridge. He didn't need the human. She was weak and he'd ordered her to rest. No way did he plan on waking her.

A quick trip to his cabin and he was changed into something more suitable to work in the engine room.

He made it to level one and exited the lift—coming to an instant halt at the sight before him.

Mari was already there, carrying the toolbox he'd recently put away. She turned, staring at him.

He took in the fact that her hair hung loose instead of in a rope of braids. It tempted him to touch it. Would it be as soft as it looked? He imagined running his fingers through those long strands. It made her appear even more attractive, showcasing her delicate features and large brown eyes. She also wore a clean version of the same outfit he'd seen her in half an hour before.

"I didn't call you."

"The computer alerted me to the problem." She dropped her gaze.

"You're not needed. I'll find the problem and fix it. Wait until you have proper gear. Pod Two will outfit you first thing in the morning."

She bit her lip and finally lifted her head, holding his gaze. "I can think of three reasons why a power surge would happen, one that could shut down the engines. What would they be?"

"You're questioning me?"

She tucked her chin fast, dropping her focus to the deck between them. "What I meant is, do you have a guess what might have caused the power surge that killed the engines? I have three."

He stalked past her into the engine room and walked to the computer relay, pressing his fingers to the screen. It lit up, and he ordered the computer to run diagnostics to find the problem.

Mari came into the room behind him and set her toolbox down. "It would have already shown the problem if the computer was able to tell us what went wrong." She moved away, crouching near a floor hatch and opening it.

He watched her turn on a flash beam, running it over all the breakers located there. "Are any blown?"

"No." She closed the hatch and stood, moving around to one of the large shafts.

"What are you checking next?" He followed.

"The genpower regulator. It could send a surge through the system if there's a short or a leak. Cross your fingers. It's an easy fix."

He watched her withdraw a tool from her pocket and begin to open the seal on a round, thick tube near the bulkhead. "If it's not?"

"I hope we have spare parts. It could be the power cuplet that runs the engines. That would be really bad if the surge happened there. I can do a workaround to get us going again, but it would mean replicating small parts and at least six hours to make a temporary repair. Those parts wouldn't hold for more than a week, and any speed over flash two would be too much for replicated metal to withstand. We'd have to return to the station we just came from to get specially coated ones from them."

He frowned, not liking that idea. He drew closer, watching her remove the top of the tube and flash her light inside again, bending a little to reach inside. "You're not wearing gloves."

"I know. It's hot but not burning. Shit. Everything looks fine."

He moved even closer, watching her lift some of the wrapped cables inside to view the circuits underneath. They were all lit, none dark or showing signs of damage. There was also no hint of a coolant leak. Minutes passed as she inspected the unit.

She rose up and turned, almost slamming into him. He backed off.

She moved past him, went to the toolbox and got more tools. He watched as she shoved them in the many pockets of her dull gray outfit, and then she began to climb a ladder beyond the backside of the massive engines.

He softly growled, following her up. "Your hair is free. That's dangerous."

"The engines are down. No moving parts to worry about. And I'm just checking the cuplet."

He wasn't even sure what a cuplet looked like, not that he'd admit it. She reached the top, and the crawl space beyond, and disappeared. He made it to the top of the ladder and hesitated to join her in the small space. It was little more than five feet wide and high.

He stayed on the ladder, watching her crawl, attempting not to stare at her ass. The outfit molded tight to her bottom since she was on her hands and knees.

"What can I do?" He hated feeling useless.

"Just stay there. It won't take long to open the panel and get a looksy inside."

"Looksy?"

She muttered something he couldn't hear. "Sorry, sir. I'm not used to being supervised while working. Looksy just means I'm inspecting the parts inside. In this case, the cuplet."

He hesitated before finally asking, "What's the cuplet?"

"It's where the power reaches both sections of the engines. If it blows, no power can reach the engines. It would explain why they both went down at the same time."

He hoped that wasn't the problem.

She stopped and twisted to sit on her ass. It was dark except for the flash beam she held between her shoulder and bent head. He heard a small motor come on and bolts hit the metal floor as she opened a panel.

"A cuplet sounds like a stupid name for a part."

She chuckled. "I didn't name the parts. Engine designers did. It's an enclosed section though that runs between the engines to send out power to each of them at the same frequency. Since both of them shut down at the same time, the problem *has* to be here since it wasn't the first two thing I checked."

He heard her grunt as she shoved the panel aside and it hit the floor hard. It sounded heavy. She pushed it out of the way and leaned in the now open section.

He was instantly worried. "Is it right there or could you fall into one of the engines?" He'd never opened that panel, or even been inside the crawl space.

"It's right here. I need to focus. Sorry, sir."

"Dovis," he reminded her.

Minutes passed. He could hear her working, thumping around, and then she crawled in more until half her body was no longer in sight. More minutes passed.

She suddenly jerked and a loud bang sounded.

"Shit!"

He began to crawl into the tunnel. "Are you hurt?"

"No. We're in trouble!" She backed up and twisted in the tight space, facing him on her hands and knees. Her eyes were wide and she looked whiter than normal.

He stopped, half inside the crawl space. "We need to replicate the parts you mentioned?"

"It's not the cuplet. The U coupling has been shattered. Shit! Shit! Shit!"

He blinked. "I don't know what that means."

She started crawling toward him. "I've seen this only once but heard about it often. Tell me this ship has weapons. You need to alert the crew. We're about to be attacked."

He pulled his upper body out of the crawl space and scowled. "What are you talking about?"

"Move! Alert the crew! Are you listening to me? This was sabotage!"

Shocked, he began to climb down. "Explain fast—right now."

She popped out of the crawl space and reached up, grabbing a bar above, and then swung around, putting her feet on the ladder. "The Raxis rigged this surge to happen on a timer. My guess? They also put a tracker on us and will show up soon to steal this vessel. Those bastards must have done it while you were docked at my repair station."

He reached the floor and waited until she was within reach, then grabbed her hips and pulled her off the ladder. She yelped. He took a step over to the wall and turned her in his arms, pinning her there. "What in the hell are you talking about?"

"The Raxis are a really shitty race of aliens known for pirating ships. Last year, we had a crippled ship reach the station. They had two shuttles, which they were able to use to haul their vessel. The Raxis had done this same thing to their ship. Fortunately for the crew, the ship was heavily armed and they managed to fight them off. Raxis usually kill any survivors and then claim salvage rights.

"Do you understand? They're going to attack us soon and kill us to steal this ship. They rig the engines to die once you get far enough away from a station, without help nearby, where it's easier for them to attack. U couplings are made of Pelsis metal. To shatter it like that, they had to send a signal to specifically target the U coupling. It kills the engines when it breaks. Shit! They're coming after us."

He set her down on her feet but kept hold of her. The smell of her fear almost choked him. "Perhaps this U coupling just failed. It happens."

She gawked up at him. "You're wrong. This *never* happens unless it's on purpose. There's only one thing that causes Pelsis metal to disintegrate. The Raxis invented a machine that can emit a vibration signal. It breaks down *only* that specific metal. I'd stake my life that one of those devices is currently attached near the engines on the exterior of the hull, and probably still sending out the frequency that did the damage. We're about to be attacked!"

He studied her eyes. They were wide, panicked, and she reeked of fear.

He believed her.

"Fuck," he snarled, releasing her and running to the computer access panel, turning on ship-wide comms.

"We have incoming pirates planning to attack! Everyone report to stations. This is *not* me fucking around. Get your asses up and prepare for battle!"

Cathian responded first, privately. "What's going on?"

"Ever heard of Raxis pirates? Your mechanic said they attached some device that caused our engine troubles, she's seen this before firsthand. No other ships were in scan range when I left the bridge but that was almost half an hour ago. If she's right, we're going to be under attack."

"Damn it. This is Cathian," the captain announced, going to full-ship comms. "Get your asses up and strap on every weapon you have."

He started to issue orders as Dovis turned, spotting Mari on her knees in front of her toolbox. She tore open drawers, seeming to search for something. "What are you looking for?"

"I can rig a fix to run the engines for a little while. Someone needs to go outside, find the tracker they must have tagged us with, and stop it from transmitting our location. Then we hope I can keep the engines up long enough for us to reach a colony planet or another station. No way can we make it back to my repair station. It's too far."

"Do what you can."

He ran out of engineering, grabbed one of the emergency comm wrist straps, and messaged Cathian. "I'm suiting up to search our outer hull for a tracking device. And maybe the device that caused the damage. Mari is working on getting our engines back online."

"I've just reached the bridge," his friend responded. "She's right. We have company coming. Two shuttles just showed up on long-distance radar. I've got York manning weapons and Marrow is sending a message to our allies that we need help. Raff is guarding the main docking door in case they try to attach and breach if we can't keep them back. Nara is heading to help Mari. Pods, scan minds and tell us if anyone is coming at us cloaked from our scans."

Dovis tried to calm his rage. "Mari believes she can get our engines running, but not for long. See who can meet us fastest and head towards them once she gets us back online. I'll kill the tracker if I find it to prevent them from following."

Chapter Four

Mari wiped the sweat from her forehead, glad that she'd at least tied her hair back. Nara had been nice enough to bring her a wrist comm unit to make communicating with the rest of the crew easier as she worked.

The crawl space was tight, hot, and airless. Cleaning out the shattered pieces of the U coupling had been difficult but was now completed. She inserted the one she'd fashioned from inferior metal and asked Nara to bring her the thickest protection gloves she could find. They were huge on her hands…she just hoped they'd be enough to keep her from dying.

The sound of blasts had started minutes before. *The Vorge* was firing at the two approaching Raxis shuttles, attempting to keep them at a distance. No help was in range enough to come to their defense right away. They were on their own for a while.

So far, the Raxis hadn't returned fire. They wouldn't want to damage the ambassador-class ship. That would negate the entire reason for inventing the little machine that took out U couplings. Most ships needed that part, and they were all made from Pelsis metal. The Raxis probably kept a box of spares on their shuttles to make the repair, giving them a completely undamaged stolen vessel to sell.

She reached up, wiping her brow again with the sleeve of her shirt, and carefully coated the pieces of metal that linked the two brackets she'd used to form a new U coupling. It wasn't pretty but it should work. The comms kept her updated on what was happening.

"They're dodging my fire but they aren't getting any closer," York stated.

"Watch power levels," Cathian warned. "Those bastards might be trying to wear down the batteries of our weapons and then come at us. Life signs say there are over twenty of those pricks between both shuttles. We'd be outnumbered if they breach us. Report, Pods. Anyone trying to sneak up on us with shielding suits on?"

"No," One stated. "We're only picking up the crew." He paused for seconds, then, "Mari, it's too dangerous. You should have told our captain that you could possibly die getting the engines back online and giving us a chance to flee this battle."

Crap. She bit her lip, wrapping padding around the now coated metal. *We're all going to die if we don't get out of here. What's one life compared to the entire crew?*

"Your life is as valuable as ours," One replied. "Captain, she's at risk of being electrocuted, even while wearing gloves to hold the parts together when we restart the engines."

"What's he talking about, Mari?" The captain's tone made her flinch.

She kept working. "It should be fine."

"She's lying," one of the Pods stated. "She is thinking she will probably die. The U coupling she has created will hold together once the power is flowing thru it, but it must be held in place at first, until a solid connection is made. The gloves won't fully protect her from being electrocuted."

A snarl sounded over the comms. She wasn't sure if it was the captain or Dovis. He'd been silent since locating two devices near the engines on the outer hull, and removing them. It was possible he was still making his way back inside *The Vorge* or was removing his spacesuit.

"It doesn't matter if I survive or not. We need to get the engines back online to recharge weapon batteries that have almost been depleted. It should give the crew a chance to lose those pirates, but very worst case, you'll be able to fight them off longer until help arrives. Raxis pirates don't take hostages or prisoners. They kill crews." Mari finished the wrap and sprayed sealer over the temporary U coupling. "The important thing is, if the part works, you can max out on speed but keep it steady, whatever you do. Any powering back might pop the coupling connection loose and the engines will go back down. Understand?"

There was silence over the comms.

The captain finally spoke, his voice grave. "Thank you, Mari. Is there anything we can bring you that would help alleviate the risk?"

"No. The gloves are the only thing small enough to wear and still allow me to fit my hands inside the hole where the coupling goes, and I have to physically push it down when you restart the engines to hold it in place for a few seconds."

"What about using a tool?"

She glanced at the toolbox a few feet from her, knowing the contents. "Any other metals might fry the cables on either end if it creates a feedback shock, and nothing else could withstand the electric current that's going to be thrown off whatever touches the coupling. It's best if I physically hold it in place."

"You're saying you're going to be holding on to a live wire?" That was Nara, and she sounded shocked.

Mari debated her words carefully. "Pushing against it to hold it in place is more accurate. The coupling I created isn't a perfect match, which means it could pop out of place when the engines start. Someone has to hold it there until the electric current is flowing." Mari paused. "Just in case I can't tell you later, thank you for hiring me. Freedom was wonderful. There's no family to notify if I don't make it."

Another snarl sounded over the comms, this one louder, almost vicious, but otherwise, no one said a word.

The captain finally came back on. "How long until it's ready, Mari?"

She swallowed hard and put on the gloves, picked up the coupling, and leaned into the open panel. "I'm installing the coupling now. Give me a few seconds and then be ready to start the engines on my go. I'll tell you."

She used her knee to push one of her tools out of the way to keep all metal from touching her except what was in her gloved hands. She's already removed everything from her pockets. The flooring and access panel were now coated as well, to ground them.

A low grunt came from her left but she ignored it. She released one side of the coupling and grabbed the metal comm unit on her opposite wrist, placing it away from her.

Then she placed both hands over the coupling again and pushed down as hard as she could.

"Restart!" she yelled.

She closed her eyes, knowing it would hurt. Her body tensed. There was a hum…

And then pain raced up both arms and beyond as power surged through the U coupling and into her body. She would have screamed but she couldn't.

The unit powered on and the engines engaged. She was aware of that as she fought to breathe but failed. Too much energy pulsed through her body. Agony had her seeing spots before she blacked out.

Dovis watched helplessly as Mari collapsed inside the panel.

He hadn't made it to her in time.

He dove for her lower body to break her connection to the coupling. Electricity shot up his arm when he touched her. He clenched his teeth, ignoring the pain. The momentum of his dive tore her free and they landed in a heap outside the panel.

The worst pain faded in seconds, leaving the arm hooked around her hips throbbing. Mari was curled in front of him on her side.

He had to use his other hand to roll her to her back in the cramped space. He managed to back up, dragging her body past the open access panel and down the crawl space. She wasn't moving, and worse, he couldn't hear if she was breathing.

"Mari, report!" Cathian's tone demanded an immediate answer.

"She's down," Dovis shouted. "I'm taking her to the medical android."

"How bad is it?" Nara sounded worried.

He stopped pulling on Mari and crawled up her body, getting closer to her face. He put his palm on her chest, feeling her soft breast underneath. Long seconds passed

She wasn't breathing...and he didn't feel a heartbeat.

"Fuck!"

"Dovis?"

"Not now, Cathian! I'm trying to save her."

But she was already gone. He'd arrived in time to see her die.

An image of her flashed through his mind, looking fearful as she'd stared up at him when he'd caught her doing repairs while she should have been sleeping. For York's steam, of all things.

The human was a sweet little thing. Gentle. Strangely pretty...and he realized he'd felt protective of her earlier that evening.

The same instinct surged again.

He refused to let her life slip away forever.

It was forbidden, against the laws of his people, but fuck them. They'd never done anything for him except make his childhood a living hell until he'd escaped his own planet.

He pinned her body between his spread thighs, tearing her uniform at the neck to get access to her shoulder.

He didn't hesitate. His fangs sank into her flesh and her blood touched his tongue. The rich flavor of it instantly made his body react in ways he didn't expect. He loved the taste of her. Heat flared through is veins until he broke out in a sweat.

He drank for long seconds, releasing his saliva into her in turn, before freeing his fangs and straightening a little, putting his muzzle near her lips.

Her eyes were closed and she didn't react in any way as he watched.

"Come on," he growled.

He had to shift to skin to breathe into her mouth, and he did chest compressions to try to restart her heart. It was possible it wouldn't work. He'd never tried to save a human. The last time he'd bitten someone, it had been Cathian's blood relative.

There'd been nothing to lose, since Raff had lay dying. It had worked without any consequences. He hoped for the same result again. Raff had begun to heal immediately, his stab wounds closing within a minute. Then again, Raff's heart had been beating at the time. Mari's wasn't.

Dovis continued to work on her—and her mouth suddenly opened, her body jerked, and she gasped in air.

He glanced down at the bite, watching it heal.

Dovis almost smiled as he shifted back to fur. The little human should be fine. She didn't wake right away, though. He backed down her body, grabbed her ankle, and dragged her toward the ladder. Her limp body slid along the floor, her arms dragging over her head, tangled with the hair she'd tied in a loose knot, which was now coming free. He exited the access tunnel and got on the ladder.

"Hurry up!" Nara yelled from below. "I have the lift waiting. Seconds count. I sent the Pods to get the medical android online and they'll be waiting."

"She's breathing," he called out. "She'll be fine. She's just unconscious."

He released Mari's ankle and grabbed her thigh, being careful with his claws as he dragged her closer. He hooked one of her arms and managed to carefully drape her limp body over his shoulder. He climbed down the ladder with her. Mari didn't weigh much but the climb was awkward.

"Come *on*," Nara urged. "We've got to get her to sick bay."

"She has no need for the android." He got to the bottom and faced Nara. She looked upset.

"Take her to sick bay *now*, Dovis! You might not give a shit if she lives but we do! That's an order." She pointed toward the door.

He couldn't allow the android to run tests on Mari. It would be proof of what he'd done to save the little human's life. "Cathian?"

"Yes, Dovis."

"Tell your life-lock to back off. I took care of it. Mari is going to be fine…it's like Max station. I'm taking Mari to her room."

Cathian paused for a long moment then spoke. "Let him go, Nara."

"But Cathian, she's hurt! He's got Mari slung over his shoulder and she's not moving."

"Nara, Dovis knows what he's doing."

"But—"

Dovis ignored her and headed out. "Are the Raxis following us?"

"Damn straight they are," York snorted. "We're leaving them behind though."

"You heard Mari," Dovis reminded the crew. "Don't power back our engines. They'll fail. I'm going to put her inside her cabin and then I'll come to the bridge."

He reached the lift. Nara ran in too, glaring at him. He pressed the button for the level Mari slept on.

"She needs to be seen by the medical android."

"Not anymore. She'll be fine."

"Sometimes I hate you, Dovis. You want to take over everyone's job, but you're not a medical android. There's no telling how badly Mari is hurt. She's out cold."

"She's breathing and has a heartbeat now. She didn't before." The lift stopped and he stormed out.

Nara stayed on his ass. "Come on. Stop being a dick. Take her to the android."

He overrode access to Mari's cabin and blocked the door, keeping Nara back until it closed with her still in the corridor. He spun, carrying the female over his shoulder to her bed then gently bent, using his hands to protect her head and back as he lay her flat. He checked the bite again. His fang marks had completely sealed over. Some blood remained. He glanced at her face briefly before leaning in and licking it away.

It annoyed him that he liked the way her skin tasted. Her flesh was sweet.

Mari made a low sound. He backed off and adjusted the torn shirt to cover her shoulder

She opened her eyes and blinked, looking dazed.

"You're fine," he told her in a hushed tone. "Rest. The engines are online and we're fleeing the Raxis pirates. You did it."

She smiled. "I'm not dead."

He couldn't help baiting her a bit. "Are you sure?"

"Yes."

"Some would think they were in hell, waking to see my face."

"*I* don't think so."

He paused, staring at her. She didn't find him ugly? Frightening? It must be a side effect of what he'd done to her. "Relax. Stay in bed for at least an hour. That's an order. You're healing, and it will take that long or longer for you to be back to one hundred percent."

She looked confused. "You gave me one of those super-healing shots I've heard about? I feel weird."

Dovis hesitated but decided the lie was best. "Yes. Exactly that. Stay in bed, Mari. I'm going to order the computer to monitor you. You move, I come back…and you don't want upset me."

"I'm tired." She closed her eyes and her breathing immediately slowed in sleep.

He straightened and walked to the door after giving the computer orders to notify him if Mari got up or if her life signs were in danger.

Nara paced in the corridor. He raised his hand to cut her off when she opened her mouth, keeping her quiet until the door closed behind him. "There are things I refuse to explain to you. Mari will be fine. Give it an hour and she'll never know she was hurt."

"You're not a doctor. Do you even have medical training?"

"I don't need training."

"What the hell does that mean?"

He strode toward the lift. "I'm needed on the bridge. Mari is sleeping. Leave her be. The rest is needed."

"Dovis, answer me!"

"Learn to trust the crew, Nara. Mari is one of us now. I wouldn't purposely hurt her."

"You're such an asshole!" she seethed. "Tell that to Harver. Oh yeah, you can't—because you beat him up until he quit!"

He was grateful when he reached the lift and it closed, blocking anything else Cathian's life-lock might have yelled at him.

Things were calm when he reached the bridge. York grinned from his station.

"We're leaving the bastards behind. Their shuttles are slow."

Cathian stared at him grimly. "You have a little blood around your mouth."

"Shit." York turned in his chair. "What happened? Did you get yourself with your teeth?"

"Something like that." Dovis wiped his mouth and moved closer to Cathian, lowering his voice. "The little human will be fine."

"Thank you for what you did. I know it's taboo."

"She's important to you." He wasn't about to admit he had panicked when he'd realized Mari wasn't breathing and no longer had a heartbeat.

Cathian gripped his shoulder and gave him a squeeze. "Still. I owe you."

"Never. We're friends. What's the situation?"

"We're leaving the pirates behind. Grover station is sending out a patrol to meet us and, if necessary, haul us in if our engines go down again. We're at a speed that will allow us to intersect with them in seven hours and six minutes. Mari saved the day." Cathian hesitated. "Do you think she helped them? The pirates? It's a little odd that I hired her and then we were attacked."

The idea didn't sit right with Dovis. "She died restarting our engines. If that was her plan, it was a shit one. She would have just sat on her ass, waiting for her friends to attack."

Cathian nodded. "I had to ask. I was sure you'd be suspicious of her. But her personality isn't that of someone who'd betray us."

"I might not like that she's here but she put her life on the line for the crew, and I doubt your android would have been able to save her. I suspect the damage she sustained was too great. She smelled like cooked meat."

His friend flinched. "Good thing you have miraculous healing abilities."

"Let's change the subject." He hated to talk or even think about what made him different from most of his own race. His people abhorred him. Shunned him. Made him an outcast.

He left Cathian's side to watch the enemy on radar. They were increasing the distance between them. The Raxis shuttles weren't built for speed and they had sustained some damage from York firing on them. He almost wished they'd boarded *The Vorge*, giving him a chance to kill every bastard who thought they could hurt his crew.

His mind kept returning to Mari. The taste of her blood still lingered on his tongue, and he was uncomfortably aware of the state of his dick. It was semi-hard.

He didn't know if he should be horrified or worried that he found her sexually appealing. She wasn't his type. Too fragile, small, and nonaggressive.

He tapped the screen to his left, pulled up security feeds, and overrode privacy protocols to check on Mari inside her cabin. He could have just viewed her vitals...but he wanted to see her.

The vid view showed that she lay on her bed sleeping, in the same position he'd left her. Her chest rose and fell as he watched.

"Breaking rules of privacy? I'm shocked, Dovis."

Cathian's soft whisper made him startle. He'd been unaware that his friend was walking up behind him, too focused on the human.

"I'm just making sure Mari is staying down. I told her to remain at rest for an hour. Her body needs to heal, but she might *feel* fine even if she's not yet. My saliva seems to give off a mild high."

Cathian chuckled. "I remember. Raff was actually talkative and nice while he healed. Laughing even. It was almost like he'd drank a lot of booze."

Dovis nodded. "She's tiny and not Tryleskian. I have no idea how she'll react. It's why I activated the vid feed into her cabin."

"Understood." Cathian hesitated. "You looked upset. Why?"

He hesitated. "Something strange happened when I bit her."

Cathian crouched next to his seat, bracing his arm along the top of the console. "What?"

Dovis hesitated.

"We're best friends. No secrets or lies are between us. I've told you everything about myself. Talk to me."

Dovis glanced back, making sure York remained at his station across the bridge. The Parri male had good hearing, but not if they kept their voices low enough. "My fangs throbbed while I bit her, and I felt…" He didn't want to admit it.

"Tell me." Cathian leaned in closer.

"You know of my childhood. I was abandoned by my parents after my mother birthed me. It's shameful to be born in skin, like I was. It proved I was flawed, one of the unfortunate ones."

"That's bullshit," Cathian growled. "Your people are fucked up for that."

"Rarely do abandoned infants survive. They starve to death, or succumb to the elements, or are killed by animals. But there was an elder female who cared for me until I was old enough to fend for myself. Her mate had died and they'd never had children. The other villagers shunned her for rescuing me, giving me food and letting me sleep inside her home on a mat. She tried to convince them she treated me like a pet, and I suppose in some ways she did. But she also told me myths about ones like me, and why we were hated."

"What kind of myths?"

"In my culture, it's against the law to use my ability to heal by saliva and bite. I was four when I first learned I had it. Taznia had fallen, she was very aged, and she'd sliced open her arm badly. She couldn't get it to stop bleeding and no one in the village would help her because she was kind to me. Instinct took over, and I began to lick her wound. The bleeding stopped and the wound sealed."

He paused, gathering his memories. "She made me swear to hide what I could do. Warned me that the others would kill me if they found out. She told me it was a death offense because those like me not only had the ability to heal, but to force others to be sexually drawn to them. Something in my saliva could make me desirable enough to take away free will."

Cathian's eyes widened. "Ever test that out?"

"Never. Before today, I'd only bitten Raff, and helped Taznia that once. She made me swear to never do that again for her. I kept my word. Even when she got sick and died."

"Raff didn't try to hump you, did he?" His friend grinned. "That would have been amusing to see."

"He didn't." Dovis scowled. "That's not funny. I actually worried about it, but he just seemed drunk."

"What are you concerned over then?"

"When I bit Mari, it was different. My body reacted to her in a way it shouldn't have."

Cathian opened his mouth but closed it. He finally asked, "You became aroused?"

"Yes."

A small smile played at his friend's lips.

"Don't. It's not amusing."

"You think humans are weak and ugly. I told you there's something amazing about Nara. She turns me on like no one ever has. Don't feel ashamed if Mari sent blood to your shaft."

"When Mari woke, she smiled at me."

Cathian looked even more amused.

"Stop. What if the myth is true, and Mari now feels sexually drawn to me? Perhaps it didn't happen with Raff because he's male."

Cathian stood. "You worry too much, Dovis. She's a small alien, you can handle her. What you did was a good thing. We'll keep an eye on her." He glanced at the screen with a smirk. "Or *you* will. She's alive. That's all that matters. We'll deal with it if there are any consequences."

Dovis nodded.

"What are you two whispering about over there?"

Dovis looked back, meeting York's curious stare. "We're discussing if you need training drills on weapons. You didn't blow up those shuttles when you should have."

York snorted. "My orders were to keep them back, not blow them to hell. Accomplished!"

Chapter Five

Mari awoke feeling terrific and refreshed. Memories of what happened flashed through her mind as she sat up. That's when she noticed her shirt was torn at her shoulder.

She frowned, wondering how that had happened. Maybe when someone from the crew had dragged her out of the crawl space? It was a tight fit in there, over the center of the engines.

She slid out of bed and entered the bathroom, using it and taking the time to get clean. Once dressed in a fresh outfit, she left her cabin, hunting for another crew member to see what was going on.

She ran into Midgel when she entered the dining room. The alien was extremely shy but nice. "Are we safe from the pirates?"

Midgel nodded. "We've met up with others and the engines are still running. I heard they'll have the part we need at the station we're heading for. How are you?"

"I'm good. Hungry. Do you mind me having some leftovers? I didn't feel like using the replicator in my room. Your cooking is much better than what those produce, even if it's cold. I know it's not yet mealtime."

"You got the engines working, Mari. I'll make you something."

"You don't have to go out of your way."

"I want to. Sit."

Mari smiled and took a seat. Midgel disappeared into her kitchen. No crew were allowed back there unless a repair was needed. Nara had told her Midgel guarded her cooking space as if it were a horde of treasure.

Ten minutes later, the shy woman returned, carrying a plate of cooked meats and vegetables. It smelled delicious.

"Thank you."

"You're welcome." Midgel rushed away after bringing her a drink, and didn't return.

Mari ate and put her empty dishes in the cleaner near the kitchen, going to the engine room next. No one was down there. She climbed the ladder, entering the crawl space. The panel remained opened and she peered inside, memories of being shocked until she blacked out first and foremost in her mind. It had hurt badly.

The U coupling she'd rigged remained in place, blue energy flowing over it. She backed away, crawled out, and decided to leave the toolbox there, since she'd have to replace the part soon anyway.

Next she went to maintenance—staring in shock at her open locker and the new outfits that hung inside. They weren't just for work, but also for off times.

Dovis had said he'd have a jacket and other things made for her. He hadn't lied. Even the fire suit looked to be her size. It was shiny, and the nicest, most expensive garment she'd ever owned. It was work related but that didn't matter. That suit could save her life one day.

She blinked back tears. The crew cared about her.

"Mari, this is Captain Cathian. We're in the dining room waiting for you to join us. Report now."

She started at hearing his voice going ship-wide through the speakers. She spun around, rushing toward the nearest lift. She wasn't wearing a comm; had he been trying to contact her for long? He sounded rather angry.

She ran when she arrived on the dining-room level and rushed inside, slightly out of breath. Captain Cathian stood inside the door with his arms crossed over his broad chest, a stern expression on his face. Nara stood next to him with an equally unpleased frown.

"I'm so sorry."

He suddenly grinned. "For what? Saving our asses?"

He stepped out of the way, and she realized the entire crew had gathered inside the dining room. Even the silent Raff, who never spoke to her or looked her way, had come. They were all staring at her, including the Pods.

Nara came forward. "You can't miss your party."

"My what?" She was stunned.

"We're celebrating not being boarded by pirates because you saved the day!"

"It was technically still night," Marrow called out. "My ass was sleeping until I was woken. She saved the night and *then* the day."

Mari didn't know what to say except the truth. "I was just doing my job."

"You did more than that." Nara kept hold of her, leading her toward the tables where the crew sat. "I asked Midgel to make you a cake."

"I've never had a cake before."

Nara froze, staring at her with wide eyes, and then her bottom lip trembled. "*Never*? What about your birthday parties?"

"There were no parties. Why would I get cake for my birthdays?"

Nara released her and pointed to a seat. "I'm getting you a drink. Me too. A strong one." She stormed off, muttering something under her breath.

Marrow asked, "Why do you want to hunt down her parents and kill them?" Her gaze tracked Nara.

"You suck at girl talk, remember? Just seal your lips. I said that low so Mari wouldn't hear me. Thanks for broadcasting it."

Marrow frowned, looking at York. "What did I do?"

York snorted. "We all hate your parents, Mari. You should know that."

She shrugged, not offended. "I don't like them either." It was no secret that her parents had sold her to the Teki.

"Sit," Captain Cathian ordered.

She took a seat by York. He was friendly and always nice to her. "You did good, Mari."

"Thank you." She was slightly embarrassed by all the attention. Her gaze drifted to Dovis in the corner. He sat away from everyone, much like Raff did. More flashes of memory returned…of him leaning over her, telling her to stay in bed.

Had that really happened? She wasn't sure. If not, it was odd that she'd dream about Dovis.

Midgel came out of the kitchen with a large, white round thing. The scent of fruit filled the room as she set it down on the table, smiling at her. "Berry cake. It's a favorite of the crew. I hope you enjoy it."

Mari stared at it, unsure what to do.

Nara returned with two glasses, placing them down, and took a long knife from Midgel. The shy cook fled, returning with more silverware and small plates. Mari watched as Nara cut the round food into slices and put them on plates, shoving one her way. Mari picked up a fork and took a tiny bite.

Sweetness and the bright taste of berries flooded her mouth.

"This is good!"

"Cake always is. When is your birthday? You should get one every year."

Mari shrugged. "I don't know. My parents never told me or mentioned a date I was born."

Nara opened her mouth but then closed it, looking angry again.

"We can assign her a date," Captain Cathian said gently, taking a seat next to Nara. "Calm, Nara. Your face is doing that red thing that makes me worry."

"Fine." Nara forced a smile. "The day you were freed can be your official birthdate now. Every year, we'll celebrate it with a cake. *Lots* of it, to make up for all the years you missed. Do you know how old you are?"

She shook her head. "No. Maybe twenty-five? I'm not sure."

Nara growled.

It surprised Mari. "I didn't know humans made that sound."

"I'm life-locked to a Tryleskian. I learned it."

Captain Cathian chuckled. "She even lifts her upper lip to flash smooth teeth at me if she's really irritated. It's adorable. Do you know how many years you were with the Teki?"

"No. I think about fifteen years, though. I just know for certain how old I was when I was sold. They haggled a lot over the price, and my age was a part of it. I was too young to be a sex slave for the station's brothel because it would offend some customers. Most humans the Teki buy are sent there. That's when they decided to put me in engine repairs. I was small enough to fit inside thruster shafts and they could drop me into intake pits to clean them out. I was supposed to transfer to the brothel when I turned sixteen, but K'pa, the Teki who purchased me, had noticed how much work I could do. He kept me in repairs instead. He said I was more valuable doing that work."

A snarl came from across the room. She turned her head, seeing it was Dovis. Again. He didn't look up but he seemed furious as usual.

She glanced at the rest of the crew. Their angry expressions mirrored Dovis's. She thought about how dangerous engine work was, and figured they didn't like the idea of a kid being at risk.

"I survived. I was smart and learned fast. It's only risky if you stay too long inside one of the shafts, because you run out of oxygen in your mask. It was an honor to get to stay in repairs. I didn't want to be a brothel worker." She felt no shame admitting that. "I worked twice as hard as everyone else to avoid being sent there."

Nara reached out and gripped her hand. "No wonder you were willing to give your life for ours. You poor thing. You don't realize how important you are. Well, that shit has changed. You're part of *The Vorge* crew now. You matter, Mari. No more crazy stunts like what you did this morning." She shot a glare in Dovis's direction. "Someone will stop you next time."

"I arrived too late," he protested. "I would have stopped her if I hadn't. She was already down when I reached her and hauled her out of the shaft."

"You refused to take her to the android," Nara pointed out. "Instead, you carried her to her room."

York cleared his throat. "No fighting, crew. It turned out fine. Worst case, those pirates would have boarded us and died. We're mean sons of bitches. Between me, Cathian, Raff, and Dovis, they all would have been killed. Don't risk your life again, Mari."

"What am I? Invisible? I can fight, you blue idiot," Marrow snapped. "Add *me* to that list."

"And Marrow," York grumbled. "Although she gets upset when blood gets splattered on her. I'm referring to Angus Twelve."

She growled at him. "It wasn't splatter that bothered me when you had to kill those two slavers who tried to grab me on that supply run. I had no problem with their blood. It was the head you threw at my chest! That was gross."

"I didn't mean for it to hit you. It just flew that way when I killed the slaver." York grinned.

Marrow rolled her eyes. "Fair."

"No more bickering. Mari must think we're savages." Captain Cathian chuckled. "Nobody share Raff stories." He winked at her. "Watch out for the silent ones," he whispered loudly.

Raff snorted from across the room but didn't say or respond in any other way.

Mari liked her new crewmates.

The Pods drew her attention when they turned her way, smiling.

One spoke. "They like you, too."

She relaxed and smiled, believing the Pod. She didn't think he'd lie to her.

Her gaze went to Dovis again. He'd taken her to her room? That memory of waking to find him hovering over her must be true. She needed to thank him.

Dovis dug into his food, ignoring the rest of the crew now that they'd given Mari her cake and were having dinner. He relaxed in his chair. She hadn't acted strange at all, or even paid him much attention. The myths Taznia told him must have been bullshit. He'd been afraid Mari would show him greater interest. His fears were laid to rest.

He was glad he'd bitten and healed her, though. No regrets.

The crew laughed and chatted. He glanced over at Raff, the other crew member who didn't like to socialize much. Raff had his own issues. Dovis didn't know all of them but he'd learned enough. Being the bastard son of Cathian's uncle had to be tough.

Raff looked full Tryleskian, but he wasn't. His mother had been some other alien race, a woman his father had spent his heat with while stranded on a planet for five months after a shuttle crash. Once his father had been rescued, he hadn't wanted to lay claim to her or the son she carried inside her body. The medical scans had shown only one infant. To a Tryleskian, that would come as a shock, since their females always carried between two to five infants while pregnant.

Raff had been raised on his mother's dangerous planet. When Cathian learned of him, *The Vorge* made a stop on Gluttren Four to find the now grown child. It was a total hellhole of a colony. Raff had stuck out big time, with his height and muscular body. They'd approached the male, offering him a job on the crew, and Raff had agreed, eager to escape the life of an assassin.

Dovis stood and got a second helping of dinner. He kept his attention focused on his food when he retook his seat, digging in.

It surprised him when a small hand suddenly gripped his shoulder.

He whipped his head around, staring at Mari. She frowned, her little nose flared as she sniffed—and then she shocked the hell out of him by leaning down to bury her face against his throat.

She inhaled loudly. "You smell really good."

"What the hell?" He jerked away and almost fell out of his seat, tearing away from her hold. He glared at Cathian, expecting the captain to laugh. His friend would put her up to something like that as a joke.

Instead of a smile, Cathian's mouth hung open and his eyes were wide. He appeared concerned instead of amused.

Mari stalked Dovis until his back hit the wall. Her head just came up to the top of his chest. She put her hands on him there and leaned in, sniffing again. She actually rubbed her cheek against him!

Her scent hit him when he sucked in a sharp breath. She was strongly aroused.

He grabbed her upper arms, careful of his claws, and held her back. "Cathian!"

The captain leapt out of his seat and came up behind Mari, grabbing ahold of her around the waist and hauling her away from him. "Shit."

"Shit is right." Dovis felt panicked as he looked down at Mari. She was staring up at him with a confused look but still reached out for him, trying to touch him again. He dodged her fingers.

"Why do you smell so good?" She frowned.

"*You* deal with this," he told his friend, then Dovis fled.

He ran out of the dining room and went straight to his cabin.

Pacing didn't help, so he eventually went to the computer, pulling up life signs. Cathian, Nara, and Mari were visiting the medical android.

A new worry hit. What if the android took blood tests and there was proof of what he'd done? The Amarai might hear and put a death bounty out on him. Just because they weren't known to like traveling in space didn't mean they didn't have allies from other planets.

Cathian was an ambassador for his planet. Would he feel obligated to hand Dovis over to them? No. Cathian would refuse and fight if his planet leaders demanded he do so. It would cause problems for the entire crew, though.

He snarled, shutting down the readings, and began to pace again.

It seemed like an hour had passed before his door chimed. He rushed over and opened it. Cathian waited in the hallway.

"Get in here. Why did you go see the android? Tell me you didn't have it run blood tests."

"Calm down. I had it run tests but not record anything. I'm aware why that would be a bad idea. I also had it erase the entire visit and everything it discovered. The information for the entire day has been purged, to avoid being uploaded to our database."

Dovis sighed in relief. "What did you discover?"

"You know about my race and our second hearts…"

Dovis nodded.

"A blood sample from Nara will show my DNA in her system. The same showed in Mari with yours."

He gawked at Cathian. "I'm mated to her? Is that what you're saying? That's impossible."

"Remain calm. We never ran any tests on Raff after you bit him, to hide what you had done to save his life. He might have had traces of your DNA too for a while. The android believes there are two possibilities."

He felt sick. "What?"

"Your DNA traces will eventually fade from her, or it will become permanent, the way some races do when they mate or life-lock."

Dovis snarled, turned, and walked to the wall. He punched it—hard.

"Don't destroy your cabin. I sent Raff to get his blood drawn. The android will test to see if your DNA remains in his body or not. *Not* would be good. It would mean it's faded."

He spun, staring at Cathian.

His friend had the nerve to smile. "Don't worry. If your DNA is still in Raff, I doubt he'll want to claim first mating rights to you. He prefers females, judging by the brothel choices he's made the few times he's visited them. I saw his charges to *The Vorge* account. Females only."

"That's not funny. The Amarai can only form matings with our sperm, when we're in heat. Never with a bite."

"It's a little amusing." Cathian took a seat on the top of the desk. "You knew you were different from most of your race. Maybe that's why they kill ones like you for biting. Maybe it's about more than forcing a female to feel desire towards you—you can mate by bite. Hell, you could be capable of mating to a bunch of people by bite, instead of just one. We know it makes females, at least, sexually drawn to you. Mari was highly aroused by your scent. Did Raff ever hit on you?"

"No!"

"Had you been around her at any point before you bit her? Maybe she just likes you."

"I was around her, but she only felt fear for me."

"Not any longer."

"Stop smiling. It's not funny!" He wanted to punch Cathian.

His friend grew somber. "Raff will report here when he knows the results. The android won't keep a record of his visit or test results."

Dovis paced. "What did you tell Nara? I know she was with you and Mari when you visited the android."

"I told her what you did saved Mari's life, but it meant *your* life could be in danger, that it could cause you to have a death bounty on your head. That was enough for her to agree to keep quiet about your DNA being found inside Mari's bloodstream. She asked questions of course, but I told her your secrets were your own and not my place to share."

The door chimed. Cathian got up and opened it, letting Raff in. The male entered and held Dovis's gaze. He shook his head.

Dovis sighed. "No traces at all?"

"None," Raff confirmed.

"There we go." Cathian smiled again. "Your DNA traces will fade out of Mari's system. It's just because you recently bit her." He chuckled and bumped his shoulder to Raff's. The family resemblance was obvious, with them standing close together. "I was taunting him about how you might want to claim him as a mate if you were carrying his DNA."

Raff growled low as he glared at Cathian.

"He felt just as thrilled by the concept." Cathian shook his head as he moved away from Raff. "Neither of you has a sense of humor. This will all be fine. Just avoid Mari until this reaction she has to you fades, Dovis. That shouldn't be a problem, since you hate people." He glanced back at Raff and chuckled again. "Good thing you're *not* carrying his DNA. She might have thought you smelled good enough to fuck, too."

At that, Raff turned and left his cabin.

Dovis reached up and rubbed his left ear. "Your cousin would probably have killed her. He's not a friendly man."

"Who can blame him after the life he's had? I'm glad he likes *us*."

"Are you sure he does? He rarely speaks. I never know what's on his mind."

Cathian hesitated. "He's never tried to kill any of us. I know he feels grateful to me for taking him off the hellish planet he was born and raised on. You saved his life once. York amuses him sometimes, because I've seen him smile once or twice over his antics. And Raff seems downright mellow around females.

"My uncle may have abandoned him, but his mother remained until death took her away. I went through his bags when he boarded *The Vorge*, to make sure he didn't have any drugs. Told him a medical scan for new crew was required. You know what Gluttren Four is like. I searched his bags while he was in the medical bay. I feared he might be addicted to something, but his bloodstream was clean, as were his bags. There were pictures and a few personal belongings of his mother inside. She mattered a lot to him."

"What about your uncle?"

"You know that death look Raff gets?"

Dovis knew it well, and nodded.

"I'm never letting the two of them meet. Backi deserves to die for abandoning a pregnant female. He showed zero honor by doing so. He's of my father's same litter, though. My father and the family covered it up. Gluttren Four is known for its high population of interbred races no one else wants to claim. Raff's mother is at least five different species. My father only told me of Raff's exitance in case his mother or her family ever contacted the ambassador," he pointed at his own chest, "to file a complaint that the child had been abandoned by a Vellar. It infuriated me when I learned what Backi had done."

"Did they ever file a grievance with anyone who held your position before you took it?"

"Unknown. There is no record of it. That doesn't mean anything. I told you, my family covered it up. Backi would have been embarrassed if anyone knew he'd had a son with what they consider a mutant female. Remember how my father reacted to Nara? She's only human, and not a mixed breed of various species."

"Your people are assholes...but so are mine."

"That's why *The Vorge* is our home and we're a family." Cathian smiled. "Too bad Raff's not your mate. We'd actually be related."

"Fuck you. That's still not funny."

"Just avoid Mari. I'm sure her reaction to you will fade." He walked to the door but paused, turning back to hold his gaze. "You know...you could do a lot worse than to be mated to a human. Nara makes me happy as my life-lock. Perhaps you should take advantage of her current attraction to you and keep the bond active, until you go into heat and can bond to her for good. She's a damn good maintenance engineer."

"Get out."

Cathian laughed as he left. "I'll have a chat with her about dodging you, too."

Dovis paced once more after the doors sealed, leaving him alone. He could avoid the little human. He just hoped she stopped feeling attracted to him soon.

Chapter Six

Captain Vellar made Mari take a seat. His office was nice, but it was where he held official meetings. She felt nervous and worried as she stared at him over his big desk. "Are you going to fire me?" She blurted her worst fear.

"No. Of course not."

She wanted to profusely thank him, and opened her mouth to do so. The thought of having to leave *The Vorge* was enough to give her nightmares. Slavers would snatch her up and she'd be sold back into servitude. He spoke before she could.

"You're a part of my crew, Mari. You also did a very brave thing by getting our engines working. We'll dock to the Grover station within the hour and the part will be delivered. Do you need help with the install?"

"No. It's pretty easy and basic."

"How long will it take?"

She thought for a moment. "Three hours max. I'm going to have to clean up the coupling holder first, after I rigged one to work. It'll be a mess when you shut down engines ,and it needs time to cool."

He leaned forward and braced his hands on the desk. "Can I trust you, Mari?"

"Of course you can. My life is in your hands."

That didn't seem to please him, as he scowled. "I'm not your new owner."

"My life is still in your hands. I don't know what I'd do if you were to fire me and send me off *The Vorge*. Slavers would target me fast. I know I'm weak and defenseless, but I make up for it by being a good worker. I'm loyal, too. I'd never do anything to upset you or betray your trust."

"Damn the Teki for labeling you as either of those things. Humans are a sturdy race." He rose to his feet, rounded his desk, and took a seat on the edge of it closer to her. "I'm about to tell you things you won't understand…but I can't offer you more of an explanation. I just need you to accept it and keep it secret. Not even the other crew can be told. Including Nara. Do you understand?"

"Yes. I give you my word. Until death and beyond." She bowed her head and offered her palm to him by straightening her arm.

"What the hell is that for?"

She glanced up. "To accept pain to prove my commitment."

"Fuck," he snarled. "No one on *The Vorge* will ever hurt you. Put your arm down."

She tucked it against her body.

The captain sighed. "Here's the basics. Dovis saved your life. I can't tell you how. But it's dangerous for him if anyone were to find out, and it's why you're feeling attraction toward him. It will fade, Mari. Don't ask questions. Again, I can't answer them. And Dovis won't. He's going to avoid you until the physical attraction you feel for him stops, but it's best you are aware of it. It's the result of what he did to save your life."

She remembered how she'd tried to thank Dovis in the dining hall, for pulling her out of that crawl space—and then suddenly she'd wanted to touch him. More than that. She'd rubbed up against him, the need to touch him so strong it became a physical ache. Her body had gone crazy. Nothing like that had ever happened to her before.

Her cheeks burned with heat at the memory and she dropped her gaze to her lap.

"Do you understand, Mari? Secret stuff that must remain that way. You weren't breathing and your heart had stopped by the time he reached you. You owe Dovis your life and your silence."

She forced her head up, stunned. She'd died?

The captain seemed to read her thoughts, or maybe just the shock on her face.

"Dovis is special," he explained. "Different. It's a crime among his people that he can do what he can. That's more than you need to know, and you must not ever tell anyone what happened. They might send people after him." He paused. "To kill him. We're loyal to each other on *The Vorge*. A family. We protect each other. It's why he refused to let you die. You're one of us now. Do you give me your word you'll stay silent?"

"Yes. I swear." She flashed to when she'd seen Dovis shapeshift. Did the captain know Dovis could do that? She wasn't about to ask, just in case he didn't. She figured he must though, because he said Dovis was special. She knew they were close friends. "It couldn't even be tortured from me."

The captain smiled. "You're an odd one, Mari. No one will torture you, but I'm glad you gave your promise. Just avoid Dovis and all will be fine. If anyone asks, tell them you had an odd reaction to the berry cake to explain why you acted that way with him in the dining room."

She instantly saddened. "Okay."

"What?"

She met his gaze. He seemed nice. "They won't let me have more berry cake. It was good."

He laughed. "Tell them it was the drink Nara gave you, then. I bet that was your first taste of wine."

"It was. The Teki don't give slaves any special food or drinks."

"Blame the wine. I hate the taste of it. Nara loves it but it's too sweet. There are various kinds she had me order."

"It *was* too sweet."

"There we go. We have a reason to offer if anyone asks why you practically molested Dovis." He smiled. "He can claim to have been shocked when you touched him as a reason why he didn't knock you on your ass. Not many females are attracted to him."

Her cheeks heated again. "Please give him my apologies. I don't know what happened. I've never felt that way before. Ever. It was so confusing. My body did weird things. I've been avoiding the Pods since it happened. They probably know what I was thinking and what I wanted to do."

Captain Vellar chuckled. "The Pods keep all our secrets. No worries about them. I saved them from death. They can be trusted."

She was curious but didn't ask.

"That one isn't a secret. Pods are normally protected on their planet, but sometimes a few greedy or powerful ones will sell their own kind to other alien races. Usually when the Pod family isn't well connected to a lot of others. No one raises a fuss if a small group of them disappear. Our

Pods were captured and sold to a criminal who used their abilities in horrible ways. They were enslaved. They were forced to read the minds of their master's enemies, and then had to watch them die in gruesome ways.

"Pods are gentle beings. It was incredibly difficult for them to exist that way. They were bombarded with fearful thoughts and suffering every moment they were in captivity. We were on Max station when we found them. They approached us after reading our minds and pleaded for help, having escaped their guard. I granted them safety on *The Vorge*, the criminal attacked us, we won, and now they're part of my crew, no longer tortured or kept against their will. I offered to return them to their planet but they feared being sold again. Here, they are safe and happy. As I said, the crew is a family on *The Vorge*. We protect each other."

"Thank you for telling me about them, and for saving me, too. My life on the Teki repair station would have become very difficult if you hadn't hired me."

"The Teki didn't sell you to me. He just wanted to make sure you were safe and paid well. It was a great deal for me, because your skills are amazing. We're lucky to have you."

She beamed, happy for the compliment. "Thank you."

"We're docking with Grover station within the hour. They have the part we need. Once it's delivered and you install it, you're welcome to take the rest of the day off. The station is a large one with some great entertainment venues." He paused. "They have brothels with males, I'm sure, if that's your preference. Charge anything you purchase to *The Vorge* account. We'll take what you spend out of your pay."

He stood and smiled. "Just don't blow all your creds. I'd also ask you to wear a wrist comm and one of the outfits with the patch that identifies you as part of my crew. I doubt anyone would be stupid enough to mess with you then. You could also ask to tag along with Midgel. She's always looking for a crew member to accompany her while on leave. She's shy too…but be warned, she'll drag you food shopping for rare spices."

"I don't need to leave *The Vorge*." She dropped her gaze. "I also have no need to visit a brothel. I've never… I mean…never."

The silence between them grew, and she peeked up.

He offered a small smile. "Oh. You've never had sex?"

"No. The Teki protected me well."

His expression hardened. "It's not always by force. I forget sometimes that you were a slave and how your life must have been. I take it that the other slaves left you alone?"

"K'pa let it be known he valued me as his hardest worker. The other slaves knew they'd be killed or harshly punished if they injured me. I struggled and broke free when a few of the males tried to touch me. They immediately backed off."

"I'm thankful for that."

"Me too." She hesitated. "May I ask you something?"

"Sure."

She worked up her courage and sat straighter in the chair. "You're mated to a human. I could ask Nara, but…it's about what happened with Dovis."

"I can't answer questions about Dovis."

"It's not how he did what he did to save me. It's about how I felt."

His eyes widened and he sat back down on the desk. "Ask."

"My body did weird things. Is that normal or is that only because of Dovis?"

"The feeling of being strongly drawn to him without warning...that was Dovis."

She lowered her chin, not able to look at him anymore. "My nipples got hard, and I felt wet and it throbbed between my legs. Was that also Dovis? Or normal?"

He cleared his throat slightly. "The Teki never had any talks with you about sex at all, did they?"

"No."

The captain sighed. "I'm not exactly qualified for this." He cleared his throat again. "Everything you described sounds perfectly natural for a human to experience when sexually aroused. Maybe you could mention to Nara that you've never had sex and don't know anything about it. She's suitable to have that talk with you. Just leave all mention of Dovis out of it."

"Thank you."

Captain Vellar stood once more, walking around his desk. "You can go now. The new U coupling should be delivered by York or Raff to you in the engine room soon. Let either of them know if you need assistance. Just don't call Dovis."

"I won't." She got up and fled, happy that he hadn't fired her.

The other emotion she felt was gratitude, to be a part of *The Vorge* crew.

It reminded her that she owed Dovis her life. She might not be able to go near him, but she could think of ways to repay him for saving her.

* * * * *

Dovis reached his cabin after leaving the bridge and saw a package sitting on the floor in front of his door. He frowned, sniffing the air. The faint scent of Mari filled his senses.

He bent, picking it up. Another scent came to him—and his stomach rumbled immediately. He tore open the top of the box and stared at the meat pie rounds inside. There were a dozen of them.

He accessed his lock, went inside his cabin, and used communications to contact Midgel, since she was the only one who made the pies and knew how much he loved the treat. She answered.

"What is this?"

The shy woman giggled. "Mari is building me a drawer to keep food warm and installing it later today. In return, she asked me to make your favorite cake. I made the pies instead. Are they good?"

He reached inside the box and shoved one into his mouth, closing his eyes in delight as he chewed. "Perfect."

"Enjoy." Midgel ended the call.

He swallowed and contacted her again. *"Why?"*

"Why what?"

"Why did Mari want you to make these for me?"

"I didn't ask. All that matters is I'm getting a warming drawer. It will make my life easier." She swiftly cut comms again.

He growled, eating another small pie. They were his favorite. Midgel only made them for him when she needed a favor, which was rare.

His door chime rang, and he put the box down and strode over, opening it.

Raff stood there, looking annoyed. He held out one of his precious Jorki fur blankets.

Dovis stared at it before frowning. "What?"

Raff sighed and threw it at him. He caught it. Raff pointed and said, "Yours." Then he turned to walk away.

"Wait! Why are you giving me one of your blankets? You search for them every time we're anywhere near Gluttren Four because you swear they're the softest thing in existence."

Raff swung around and stomped back. "Two words—blue lights."

Dovis frowned deeper. "I don't understand."

"I like the blue lights in the observation lounge. Mari is putting them in my cabin. Get it?"

Dovis ran his fingers over the luxurious blanket. "So...why give me one of your blankets?"

Now Raff looked annoyed. "Ask *her*. I get lights, you get the blanket." Then he sighed. "She likes you, Dovis. Don't be a dumbass. Keep her. You're as flawed as I am. It might be your only chance to have a mate."

"Her feelings aren't real. They're just because I had to bite her."

Raff stepped closer. "*I didn't want to fuck your ugly ass, and you bit me. Ditch the fur and seduce her while you have her attention, moron. I hope you're a great fuck to make up for your shit personality."*

Shock jolted through him and he reached out fast, grabbing Raff by the arm when he tried to walk away.

Raff stilled, glancing down at his hand before arching one eyebrow.

"Ditch the fur?" Dovis was alarmed. Raff shouldn't know he could shift. Cathian wouldn't betray his trust.

Raff smiled. It was a scary sight. "I survived growing up by learning everything about the people around me and finding their weaknesses and secrets." He withdrew his arm from Dovis's hold. "I put a vid device inside your vent when I first came aboard because I wasn't sure I could trust you. I've since learned I could. I haven't watched the feed since about two weeks after that, but it's got a motion sensor. I recently got a bunch of alerts. Mari has been crawling through the vents all over *The Vorge* to clean them out. She's not lazy like Harver was, only doing the outside of the grates. I watched the footage—she *saw*, Dovis. She knows you can ditch the fur. Bet she hasn't said shit about it, has she?"

He was too stunned to speak but he turned, staring at the two grates in his room that led to the vents running through the ship.

"Mari's a tiny thing compared to us. She crawls right through the vents on every level, using her clothes to catch the dust inside the ducts, and then she sprays the grates down a few times if they're bad. Hard worker. She's been doing it at night while the crew sleeps. Ex-slaves are always extreme people pleasers, her life depended on not pissing anyone off and making her owners happy. They also know how to keep their lips sealed."

Dovis faced him and tried not to show his panic. Raff and Mari had both seen too much. They knew he was a shapeshifter. "This is the most I've ever heard you say. And I'm tearing out the fucking vid device. You shouldn't be spying on anyone."

Raff shrugged. "Old habit. It kept me alive. Do you know how many times I overheard someone plotting to murder me? Too many. Lose the fur and seduce the human, Dovis. Your bite did something to her. Use it. *I* would. Didn't you notice how I stormed off after Cathian said something about Mari being attracted to me if your DNA was still in my bloodstream? I was tempted to have you bite me again just for that purpose. Unfortunately, it would only be temporary."

Dovis gawked at him.

"What? I'm fucking lonely and flawed. I wasn't born with a second heart to give to a female, like Cathian. It means I can't life-lock to one. Take advantage of what your body can do, dumbass. Shift and track her down. Mari sure as hell isn't going to want to kiss that muzzle and the pointy teeth you usually wear. Cathian and the crew would also be pissed if you scratched her with your claws. Ditch those, too, when you fuck her." He turned and walked a few steps but then glanced back, grinning. "You might be less of a shaft-head if you had a mate." Then the male walked out of sight.

Dovis backed away until the sensor triggered his door to close. He rubbed his fingers over the soft material of the blanket and sighed. How many of the crew had figured out his secret, that he could switch forms?

He snarled and walked to his couch, throwing his body down. Then he remembered the vid device and jumped up again, stalked to the first grate and yanked it open.

He found it inside the second one, cleverly hidden inside the vent. He growled, destroying the device.

One thing was certain. He and Mari needed to talk. She couldn't keep exchanging favors to get him gifts. He wasn't even sure why she felt the need. Was it because his bite made her body want him? In his culture, males perused females. Maybe with humans it was reversed. Either way, everyone would be talking about it. He didn't like being the source of gossip.

It would be smarter to use the comms to speak to her but he wanted to do it in person, to see her face and read her expressions for honesty. He'd just avoid getting too close to her. She'd been fine in the dining room until she'd approached him.

That was the key. Space.

He took a few deep breaths and then ran a scan to see where she was at that moment. He found her in engineering. The new part had come and was being installed. He would wait for her to finish and then go visit her.

Chapter Seven

Mari had just put away her new clothes in her cabin when the door suddenly opened. She twisted around to watch Dovis enter. He wore his standard black uniform. He stopped just inside the door and closed it behind him. He lifted a hand and pointed a claw-tipped finger at her.

"Stay over there. Sorry I used my security clearance to enter without permission but I didn't want anyone to see me in your cabin."

"Why?"

"That's what *I* want to know. Why are you doing favors for the crew to make them give me stuff?" He looked angry.

"I'm sorry. I thought it would make you happy."

"But why do it?"

"To thank you for saving my life, Dovis."

"There's no need. You got hurt getting the engines working to save us from being attacked by pirates. I'd have done it for anyone."

She didn't know why that made her chest ache in a painful way. "Okay." She lowered her chin and gazed at the floor between them. "I'll stop trading favors."

"How did the installation of the U coupling go?"

"Good. We're able to leave the station whenever the captain is ready. I informed him of that but some of the crew want to spend another day here, I guess."

A low growl came from him. "Look at me."

She raised her chin.

"Did you tell anyone what you saw from my vent grate while you were cleaning it?"

She felt the color drain from her face. How did he know about that?

"Did you?"

"No."

"Were you purposely spying on me? Why?"

"It was an accident. I was just cleaning the vents, I swear. I didn't even know that was your cabin. The cabins aren't marked by who they belong to."

He seemed to study her closely with his black eyes. "I believe you. What exactly did you see?"

She hesitated to answer, not wanting to infuriate him.

"Tell me," he said, taking a step forward. "You owe me that much. The truth."

"I didn't know you were in your cabin when I began to clean the grate. You stepped out of your shower. I was too afraid to crawl away in case you heard me inside the vent. Then you changed while going to sleep."

"You didn't tell anyone?"

"Never."

"Why not?"

"I'm not allowed to talk about things I see while working. I'm just to do my job. Some slaves like to gossip but I've seen them punished for it. I would never do something that earned me a lot of pain or possible death. I keep my mouth shut. You can depend on that."

"What did you think when you saw me in skin?"

"I was afraid you'd hear me and rip open the grate to tear me out of the vent if you discovered me there. I worked on a repair station for a long time. I've heard about shapeshifters before. I know this is probably your social form, but when you're alone, you wear the other one."

"I frighten you like this." He waved a hand at his body.

"You're big, and you have sharp teeth. You remind me of a race I saw once on the station. It ate another alien."

He gaped at her, blinking.

"Sorry." She lowered her gaze. "No offense."

"None taken. I promise to never take a bite out of you."

She smiled slightly and dared to look at him again. "Thank you. I appreciate that. I think I'd taste terrible and I don't have a lot of meat on me."

"You actually taste good."

Her eyes widened, surprised at what he'd said.

He cleared his throat. "Forget I said that. I just wanted to get thing cleared up between us. You don't owe me anything. Stop doing favors for the crew to get them to give me their stuff or make me things. It was nice…but there's no need."

"I'm sorry. This is all new to me. I was trying to show my appreciation."

He glanced around her cabin. "It's very clean in here."

"Of course. I will always make sure I pass inspection."

He shook his head. "No one cares if your cabin is clean or not. Ask York. His cabin is a mess. I take it your owner made you keep your cabin clean?"

"Not him directly, but one of his assistants or family members checked our living spaces almost daily. They were tiny rooms with a narrow cot. It's punishable to be messy. It shows disrespect for all we're given. Slaves should be grateful at all times."

"You're not a slave anymore, Mari."

"I know. It's just…I'm never sure how to act or what the rules are."

"I understand that. It was difficult for me when I first left my home planet. I knew nothing about other races. My first job was station security." He almost smiled—or what passed for one when the corners of his mouth curved slightly at the sides of his muzzle. "I got the job because I scared everyone. I was aggressive, figuring I needed to be to prevent anyone from messing with me. I snarled at the person who interviewed me and he grinned, thinking it was great. He asked if I could fight, and I ended up training a lot of my co-workers."

"You look very tough."

He chuckled. "Not in my other form."

"I didn't really get a good look. I was too afraid you'd find me in the vent. I just wanted to get away from you."

He closed his eyes—and she was stunned when his fur began to recede.

His muzzle shrank and bones made soft popping noises. Just as she had inside the vent, Mari watched in amazement as his ears got smaller and he changed forms. Like before, he had tan skin and full lips—but when he opened his eyes, she gasped. The black color had lightened to a soft brown.

Dovis was actually good-looking. When his muzzle had pushed in, the bones seemed to settle somehow to make his face a little wider and give him strong cheekbones.

He took her breath away.

"Still tough-looking?"

His voice wasn't as deep but remained very masculine and husky. She nodded. "You're still big and muscular. You also still look as if you could hurt someone."

He smiled. This time it was easy, and clear to see since he had a very human-like mouth. She noticed he had long, thick eyelashes. His chin was squared. It was tempting to go touch his skin to see if it was as soft as it looked. She didn't dare, though.

"I've seen a lot of aliens. You've very handsome for one. May I ask why you hide this side of yourself from the crew? I mean, if you do. I just assumed."

His smile faded and he took another step closer, but stopped. "Cathian has seen me this way. Apparently, Raff has too. This is a shameful form for an Amarain. It's rare and considered a birth defect."

"I don't understand."

"Myths on Amarai, my planet, say we're a mutation. I was born in skin and couldn't grow fur or change to look like them until what you would call puberty. My parents dumped me outside of our village after I was born, leaving me to the elements to die. It's shameful to birth one like me. An elder female found me and took me into her home. It's how I survived."

"I don't understand. Can't all of your kind change forms?"

He shook his head. "Not to this degree. They can shorten their fur and muzzles to show submission to someone more dominant but never all the way to skin. And I can do more than just change drastically in appearance." He hesitated. "I bit your shoulder, Mari. There's something in my saliva that can heal pretty severe injuries. It's also considered a shameful mutant thing. My culture is kind of into fighting and suffering. To be able to heal the way I can is considered criminal and against nature."

"Your people sound pretty dumb. It's a wonderful gift to be able to heal someone else." Then she gasped, realizing she'd said that out loud and maybe insulted him. "Sorry!"

He shrugged. "You're attracted to me because of a side effect of my bite. There was a myth the elder female shared with me, about mutants being able to draw women to them sexually with their bite. I didn't really understand or believe what she said…until you started sniffing and touching me. I apologize for that. It should stop once my DNA leaves your system. I had to bite Raff once, but he wasn't attracted to me. It must be because you're a female." Dovis cleared his throat. "Anyway, I figured you deserved an explanation if you were confused as to why you'd find me sexually appealing. You aren't losing your mind. It's just a reaction to the bite."

"I appreciate you being honest with me."

"Don't share anything I've told you."

"I give you my word. Until death and beyond." She approached him and raised her arm, presenting him with her palm, then bowed her head.

"What are you doing?"

She lifted her chin. "Giving my word. I gave my promise to the Teki before. See?" She showed him her other palm, two deep, thin scars running along its length. "I'm willing to suffer the pain of you slicing my skin to prove my commitment to keeping my silence. I won't make a sound while you cut me."

He grabbed her hand in his. His skin felt soft and hot. "I *hate* the fucking Teki. They did this to you?" He turned her hand over, examining the scars. A growl rumbled from him.

She inhaled…and once more loved the way he smelled. Better than food when she had gone too long without eating. Her body began to do funny things again, too. Her nipples beaded and an ache started between her legs. Part of her began to throb down there.

She'd forgotten to stay away from him. Mari knew she was breathing faster.

Dovis's soft brown eyes widened as they stared at each other. His nostrils flared, and his hold on her hand tightened. "Shit."

"I forgot."

Her gaze lowered to his lips, and for some reason she wanted to touch them. She hesitated for just a second before reaching up with her free hand and lightly brushing her fingertips against them. They were firm but pleasant. The texture wasn't quite like her own.

She jerked her hand back, realizing what she'd done.

"Fuck." Dovis's voice deepened. "I need to leave." He released her hand. "Now." He spun around and activated the door to open.

Mari didn't want him to go. She had freedom and a new life. She was a female human in her twenties. Last time she'd caught his scent, her body had ached for a long time. The idea of sex made her curious, and she'd seen the captain kissing Nara. It looked nice. "Stay! Please?"

He paused.

"Please stay. Will you at least kiss me?"

He faced her and took a step forward, the door closing at his back. "You don't mean that."

"I do." She stepped closer.

"You're only attracted to me because of the bite."

"Maybe...but I still want you to kiss me." He'd also saved her life. She was smart enough not to mention that to him though.

No one had really cared about her enough to break rules. Captain Cathian had implied if anyone ever found out what Dovis had done that he could be killed. Maybe he'd only taken the risk because she was crew...but she stared at his mouth, wanting to feel it against hers anyway. He was so handsome without the snout. Less frightening.

He moved closer still. "Don't hate me later. Swear."

"My promise is given."

He grabbed her waist, making her gasp at how fast he could move—and then his mouth covered hers.

Her lips were parted from the sound she'd just made, and his tongue delved inside, meeting hers.

She thought he *smelled* wonderful, but his taste was even better.

Mari moaned, clutching his shoulders. Thoughts left her mind and all she could do was feel.

Dovis kissed the hell out of Mari. She tasted sweet and his body felt on fire. The idea of shifting back to fur at that moment was something he feared, but the urge didn't surface.

He lifted Mari off the floor and she wrapped her thighs around his hips. He had to tear his mouth from hers to watch where he walked. He made it to her bed and placed her on the mattress, following her down.

He licked her throat and placed kisses there. Her little fingers were tearing at his uniform, trying to get to skin. He freed one of his arms and reached to the side of his shirt, fumbling with the hidden flap, and finally tore it open. He had to lift off her to remove the entire thing and toss it away.

Mari's eyes were wide. She panted and ran her hands along his bare chest. Her touch on his sensitive skin nearly drove him insane.

He wanted her. His shaft swelled until his uniform pants were almost painful. He stared into her eyes. "Tell me to stop."

"More," she whispered. Her hands seemed frantic as they stroked his skin from his chest to his bare shoulders. She dug her short fingernails into his skin and tried to pull him closer.

"Damn it, Mari. This is just from my saliva."

"Don't care. Please! I hurt." She released his shoulder and eased a hand between her legs. "Right there. It throbs."

He inhaled the scent of her arousal and snarled, lifting up and pulling away from her hold. She made a sound of protest but he ignored it, grabbing her little feet and tearing off her foot covers, tossing them aside. He bent, reaching for her pants next. They had one overlapping button he just tore off before yanking the material down her legs. Humans didn't appear to wear undergarments…or at least an ex-slave didn't.

She had a small bit of fur between her legs. The scent of her need was stronger minus the clothes, and he dropped to his knees, grabbed her thighs, and yanked her to the edge of the bed.

"You asked for this, Mari. Don't forget."

"What are you doing?" She tried to sit up and close her legs.

He didn't let her. Instead, he spread her thighs wider and buried his face in that little patch of fur.

The taste of her on his tongue had him snarling with need.

She moaned and her fingers plunged into his hair. She didn't try to tear him away though, as he licked and tasted her.

The hard little nub he licked made her moan louder. He remembered what he'd read about humans when he'd researched what Cathian might do to feed from Nara, after she'd been brought onboard when his friend was in heat.

He sucked and licked on her clit. He had to hold her down when she bucked her hips as if he were hurting her, but he knew better from the pleasured sounds she made. The scent of her arousal grew stronger, and then she cried out his name. The little nub he focused on began to soften slightly.

He gently stopped and released her thighs, straightening to see her face.

Mari's eyes were closed, her pale skin flush as her breathing raced.

He reached down, opened his uniform pants, and let his shaft free. Dovis gripped her legs, lifted them to rest on the his hips, and slid one hand under her waist to pull her closer. He looked down as he lined them up, until the tip of his shaft pressed against her flesh.

"Mari, are you certain?"

She opened her eyes and met his gaze. "Yes."

"I'll be careful." Humans liked facing positions, from what he'd read. He could see her expression and it would let him know if he caused her pain. She looked small down there, but he pushed against her slit. She was really wet. A groan tore from him as he aimed thick tip of himself against the slit of her pussy. He paused and then released the base of his shaft, getting a good hold on Mari's hip. He pushed in all the way in one swift thrust.

She cried out, and he lowered his upper body, pinning her under him as he took possession of her mouth. He was buried deep inside her tight sheath. Her arms wrapped around his neck, and he kissed her. She hesitated for a few seconds but then began to respond. He withdrew a little, paused, and pushed back inside her body.

He *loved* the way she felt. Wet, snug around him, and so hot. Soft even there. He thrust slow and steady, liking the way she wrapped her legs around his waist, their bodies pressed against each other. He wished he'd removed her shirt, though.

He broke the kiss, allowed his hand to shift to claws, and carefully tore open the material to see her breasts.

They were beautiful. Not too large…the perfect size. He dipped his head to taste one of her taut pink nipples. She moaned again.

He rocked his hips faster and her moans grew louder.

She felt perfect and so right. His balls tightened and he knew he was going to expel his seed soon.

Mari dug her fingernails into his back, clawing him. It increased his pleasure.

He released her nipple with his mouth. "Harder," he urged.

Her nails dug into his skin, and he knew she was probably leaving scratches along his back. He fucked her faster. Her sex tightened around him and then she threw back her head, almost screaming. It hurt his ears but he didn't care as he stopped holding back, thrusting harder.

His seed expelled, ecstasy ripping from his balls upward to his brain.

He braced his arms to keep his weight from crushing her as he slowed his thrusts until every drop of his seed was inside her. He didn't want to move, enjoying the feel of her pinned under him with her limbs wrapped around his body. Their skin touched everywhere. That felt good, too, but not as amazing as what they'd just shared.

Mari cleared her throat, and he looked down to find her watching him. She smiled. "You vibrate down there."

Her words confused him. "I don't understand."

"You were kind of growling the entire time, and it gave off vibrations." Her cheeks turned pink. "Can I see you down there?"

She surprised him again. "You want to see my shaft?"

She nodded.

He'd already shown himself in skin, and they'd bred, so he agreed. "Fine. Release me."

She hesitated but finally eased her hold around his neck and his hips. He pushed off the bed and got up from his knees on the floor to stand. Mari sat up and stared at his groin.

Her eyes widened...and he looked down.

Red blood was smeared on his shaft, which remained semi-hard still.

"Is that normal? I'm not on my monthly cycle. I would have warned you."

Her innocent question jerked him out of his shock. "No." He bent, pressed her onto her back, and spread her legs again. There was red blood on her sex now. It hadn't been there before he'd inserted his shaft. "Shit! I think I hurt you. That's not my blood. It's yours. I'd know the scent anywhere after biting you."

"It was my first time. Maybe that's why? It hurt for a split second when you entered me, but then it felt so good it didn't matter."

"You've never been bred before?"

"No."

He held out his hand. "Stand."

She took his hand and he pulled her up. He spun her away from him and wrapped one of his arms around her waist, pulling her against him. "I'm going to bite you. It will heal whatever damage I did. You were very tight." He used his other hand to move her hair from her neck, then dipped his head. She was short, but he bent low to reach her shoulder and lick her skin.

He shifted back to his other form and gently sank his teeth into her flesh.

Mari gasped, stiffening in his hold, but she didn't try to pull away. He tasted her blood, tempted to drink, but withdrew his fangs, licking at the bite before inspecting it. The puncture wounds sealed almost instantly. He leaned in again and licked away any blood, cleaning her.

Mari squirmed against him.

"Hold still."

"You're making me ache between my legs again. Throb," she whispered.

He flinched when she peered up at him. He waited for her to jerk away, since he was in his normal form, but she didn't. She seemed calm. He adjusted his hold on her waist and his claws brushed lightly over her skin, where her torn shirt gaped open. It reminded him that he'd hurt her if he took her again the way he was.

"Lay down on the bed and take off that damn shirt."

She yanked off the torn material and tossed it aside.

He hated to see the sight of blood on her thighs. He'd done that to her...but on some species, it happened their first time. She wouldn't be in any pain, now that he'd bitten her, any damage he'd done repaired.

He bent, removing his shoes and his pants as he forced the fur to recede. His jaw ached from two changes so close together, but it didn't matter. There was no way he'd risk hurting her. He crawled onto her bed in skin.

"Are you certain you want me again, Mari?"

She held his gaze, reaching for him. "Yes."

Chapter Eight

Dovis woke on his back and stared up at the cabin ceiling. They'd never dimmed the lights before falling asleep.

He was stunned. He'd bred with Mari four times, until she'd passed out. He'd just meant to close his eyes for a few moments, but he'd fallen asleep, too.

She currently dozed as she lay mostly on top of him, her head resting on his chest. One of her hands moved from time to time along his rib cage, as if she were assuring herself in her sleep that he remained in her bed. It tickled a little.

He'd never slept with a female before. Brothel workers were paid by the hour. He bred them once or twice, then left. That was the sum of his sexual history. What if Mari regretted what they'd done together?

His stomach churned…because *he* didn't.

Raff's words haunted him. Could he keep Mari interested in him if he kept biting her? Was that even fair?

He moved his hand carefully, untangling it from her long hair that spilled across her back, part of him, and over the bed. She had a lot of it, but he liked the silky texture.

Mari stirred and lifted her head. Their gazes met and she surprised him by smiling.

"You stayed."

"Did you want me to leave?"

"No."

"Are you angry over what we did?"

Her smile faded and she looked confused. "Why would I be?"

He sighed. "Mari, my bite arouses you. It could be viewed as if I'd drugged you."

"That's not true."

"It is. You only showed sexual interest in me after I bit you."

She stared into his eyes for long seconds. He prepared for the worst. For her to order him to get out and turn angry, now that he'd pointed out the truth. It was her right to accuse him of taking advantage of her. Hell, he *felt* guilty.

"I knew what your bite did to my body, but I still approached you. You tried to leave. I asked you to stay. You even kept asking me if I was certain of what I wanted every step of the way. I wasn't lying when I said yes. Don't make this into something bad, Dovis. Please?"

He gently stroked her cheek. "I feel like I didn't leave you much choice. I should have been stronger but I wanted you too badly. I'm sorry, Mari."

She rolled away from him and got out of bed, almost running into the bathroom. The door slammed behind her.

He watched her go and snarled, sitting up. "Damn it."

He stood and began to dress. He shifted back to fur and finished putting on his uniform, then took a seat on the edge of the bed. Mari took her time, but she finally came out, her hair wet and a towel wrapped around her body. She looked surprised to see him waiting for her.

"We need to talk about this, Mari."

She shook her head. "We don't. You regret what we did. I'm just an ex-slave and you're head of security. It would embarrass you if anyone ever found out you'd lowered yourself to visit my cabin, that we had sex. That's why you snuck in. I won't tell anyone." She went to offer her palm by raising her hand toward him but then stopped herself, wrapping her arms around her body instead. "You have my word."

He rose to his feet and frowned. "That's not it. I'm afraid you'll regret what we did once you have time to think about it. You were obviously saving your body for your mate."

Her eyes widened as she gaped at him. "No. That's not what I was doing."

"I'm the first male who's ever bred you. It's why you bled."

"Who was I supposed to be with? Fellow slaves? A Ricket? There was one human male slave at the station. The Teki usually only bought females. I hated him. He was older and mean. And the Teki thought I was ugly. I wasn't attracted to any of the other alien slaves. No one interested me until *you*, Dovis."

He felt confused. "Nara thinks I look like Earth's version of a dog. A type called a werewolf."

"I don't know what a werewolf is." She studied his face. "But you look good right now to me too. I admit, I'm a little worried about kissing your muzzle, though. Your teeth are sharper." She shocked him by coming closer and reaching up, gently touching his face. "Your fur is soft. Do you want me to kiss you to prove I find you attractive no matter what you look like?"

He backed away. "No. I'd hurt you in his form." He lifted his hand, showing her the claws. "Not only would kissing me be painful, but my touch would be, too."

"Oh."

"I should leave. The attraction you feel for me isn't real, Mari. It's from my bite. I shouldn't have taken advantage of you. I...I am sorry."

He left her cabin fast before he could beg her forgiveness. The hallways were empty as he made his way back to his cabin on another level without running into the crew. The Pods would probably know where he'd been. Sometimes he hated having them onboard, but they were crew. He doubted they'd tell Cathian or anyone else what he'd done.

In his room, he stripped down and showered. Messages waited for him when he checked. Cathian wanted him to undock them from the station and head toward Callon, where they needed to visit to purchase those pets the Tryleskians had asked them to buy.

He put on a fresh uniform and commed his friend.

"Were you sleeping? I assumed so since you didn't answer my hails."

He wanted to confess to Cathian what he'd done with Mari but didn't. "Yes." It was the truth. He'd gotten a few hours of sleep. "Everyone is back onboard?"

"Yes. Raff was the last to return."

"I'll go to the bridge now."

"Mari said the engines should work perfectly and requested I keep a few spare parts. I bought them."

"Good. I'd hate a repeat of what we just went through."

"I would too." Cathian paused. "Are you feeling alright? You sound off."

"I'm fine."

"Did you visit the station? York said he left you a message but you didn't answer him either. He wanted to visit a brothel and said your mood might improve if you went with him."

"No. I'm on my way to the bridge."

"We could undock in six hours if you want to go get laid first. I'm not exactly looking forward to buying a few hundred animals to transport home."

"I don't want to visit the brothel."

"Fine. Undock us and get us to Callon, then."

He left his cabin and reached the bridge. The three Pods were waiting for him. He snarled. "Great."

One blinked up at him. "Her feelings are hurt."

"You made her cry while she showered, and feel ashamed," Two muttered. "Asshole."

Three, usually the happiest of the three, just glowered at him.

"Are you going to tell Cathian or anyone else?" Dovis glanced at them.

One answered. "No. Of course not. You wouldn't really kill us. You're just in a bad mood."

"Don't tempt me. This is none of your concern."

"Mari is alone," Three whispered. "She had hope that you might have feelings for her, until you made her think you regretted what happened between you. That's not what *you* were thinking, though. You should have told her the truth. You don't want to lose her, but you fear she'll reject you if you don't keep biting her. You like her, Dovis. You have mating thoughts about her."

"She doesn't feel like you took advantage of her," Two announced. "She was aware her body did strange things around you and she was curious. Now that you've been intimate, she has other feelings."

"Strong feelings," One added. "Go to her and tell her you feel things, too. It will make her happy."

"She's not happy right now," Two grumbled. "Asshole."

He glared at the middle one. "Stop calling me that."

"You're calling yourself that. Why can't I? I just say it out loud."

"Get off my bridge and stay out of this. It's a private matter."

The Pods left but all three of them shot him dirty looks. He relaxed when the doors closed and he was alone on the bridge. He took the captain's chair and began undocking procedures, notifying the station they were leaving.

He increased speed once they cleared the station and set a course to the planet Callon. He had just taken a seat in York's normal station to watch for anyone following them when the bridge doors opened and Raff entered.

Dovis turned to glare at him. "What do you want?"

"You're a dumbass."

Anger immediately filled him. "The Pods went to you?"

"No. You removed the vid device in your cabin—but not Mari's."

He was out of the seat in seconds and lunging for Raff.

The bigger male withdrew one of his blades and pointed it at him. "Don't. Cool down. I didn't come to fight."

Dovis stopped, snarled at him, wanting to do damage to the male. "You *spied* on us?"

"Do you never listen to what I say? This is why I don't bother speaking often. I told you I usually watch someone for at least two weeks when they become crew."

"You also said Mari basically wasn't a threat."

"That doesn't mean I wouldn't keep an eye on her. You took part of my advice by ditching the fur and claws, but you were supposed to keep her. She didn't even flinch away when you got all fury before you bit her shoulder. Do you know what that tells me? You probably could have gotten away with bending her over right there and taken her before you shifted again. You're ugly as fuck right now and she *still* offered to kiss your muzzle before you left. That's got to be love, man. Get your ass back to her cabin and fix your mistake. I'll stay on the bridge and kill anyone who tries to attack us if some idiot from the station decides we'd make a good target."

"Mari doesn't know me well enough to love me. Just stop talking."

"Human females are strange creatures. Look at Nara. My cousin keeps her sexually pleased and he's nice to her. In exchange, she let him put his second heart inside her chest to life-lock with her. And she fell in love with him fast. It's probably a human thing. Not only that, she gave away her shuttle and left a career to stay with him. In comparison, Mari had a shit life before now. It's not like you have to work hard at making her happy, and you got the sexual pleasure part right. I didn't watch most of that—no offense; I didn't want to see that much of you—but it sounded like you were doing good."

He glared at Raff, still wanting to beat him up. "Get off my bridge and remove the fucking vid device from Mari's cabin, *now*."

"Dumbass. If *you* won't take her for a mate, maybe I will, once she realizes you're too stupid to waste time caring about."

Dovis fought the urge to attack again as he watched Raff put his blade away in the holster and leave the bridge. Instead, he threw back his head and roared.

He'd fucking kill Raff if he went anywhere near Mari.

* * * * *

Mari sniffed the pillow, inhaling Dovis's scent. It had been two weeks since he'd left her cabin. They'd avoided each other since. He seemed to enjoy working while the rest of the crew slept. She stayed inside her cabin during those hours.

She missed him.

He'd shown her a side of himself he'd said only Cathian had seen. That had to mean something. Or maybe she was fooling herself.

The comms dinged and she rolled out of bed, tugging on her clothes to get them righted. "Mari here."

"It's Raff. You're needed on the bridge. I think a few circuits blew on the life support control monitor. It went dark."

"I'll grab my toolbox and be right there."

"Hurry up."

"Sure thing."

She ran into Midgel at the lift. The timid cook smiled at her as she exited.

"Do you know anything about males?"

Midgel nodded. "What do you want to know?"

"How do you get one interested in you?"

"To fuck or to keep?"

Mari had to think about it. "Both?"

"Undress and show skin. That seems to work for most species. My race doesn't have mates, though. We only breed if we want to birth a litter."

Mari felt stunned. "A litter?"

"Usually six to ten." She tapped her flat stomach. "I've bred twice. I have seventeen children in all. I removed my clothes for the males both times and they jumped on me. But after, I didn't want to keep either of them. Males are a nuisance, and far worse than raising the two litters I've had. Always clinging to you, climbing on your body, and making demands."

Mari was still surprised by her revelation. "Where are your kids?"

"Grown and on their own. We're solitary creatures, once we're adults."

"Don't you ever get lonely?"

Midgel wrinkled her face, her whiskers twitching. "No. I like being alone. I'm done breeding and glad for it. Too much talking."

With that, she walked away. Mari watched her enter her cabin down the hall and then got inside the lift. "Strange woman," she muttered.

She visited maintenance first and then headed up to the bridge. She ran over possible reasons why the console would go down on the bridge but not register on *The Vorge's* computer. It should have alerted her before Raff did.

The door the bridge auto-opened at her approach. It was the first time she'd been there. It wasn't Raff waiting for her though. Dovis sat in the captain's chair.

He jumped up and spun, staring at her.

"What are you doing here?"

"Raff said I was needed." She glanced around, hunting for a dark panel. Every console appeared lit.

"Interfering asshole," he muttered.

The insult hurt her feelings. "I'm just trying to do my job."

"Not you. I'm talking about Raff. Everything is in working order." He pointed a clawed finger to his left. "See? Nothing wrong or it would show on the monitors." Dovis sighed. "He sent you up here for me."

Mari bent and placed her toolbox on the deck. "Why?"

"I've been avoiding you."

"I know."

"Are you still suffering from being attracted to me?"

She inhaled. He was too far away. She walked forward until only a few feet separated them and sniffed again. His incredible scent filled her nose and her body responded lightning quick. "Yes."

"You should back away."

She returned to her toolbox. "I guess I should go then. I wondered why the computer didn't alert me the second it went down."

"Mari?"

She turned to face him. "Yes?"

"How have you been?"

Missing you. She wasn't going to admit that, though. "Good. Working."

"I'm aware. I've been tracking your movements on the ship. You've done every repair on the list you were given and now you're overhauling things that aren't even scheduled for weeks yet."

"No complaints mean Captain Cathian will allow me to stay on *The Vorge*. I can't lose my job." It still scared her to think about what could happen if she were left on her own.

"He's not going to fire you. Harver wasn't even qualified for the job. He learned as he went. He was always downloading repair logs and having to consult with them while he worked. When asked if he knew what he was doing, he'd say 'we'll see if I can get it working.' It didn't instill a lot of confidence. You're excellent at repairing everything. Cathian stated he was lucky to have gotten you from the Teki." He made a low growl. "He threatened to collar me over you. Nara and I fight often, but he's never said he'd hand her a remote to shock me at the push of a button. Your position here is secure. More so than mine."

"I don't believe that."

"You just need more self-confidence. I investigated other Raxis attacks after they targeted us. Are you aware that you're the only engineer who's ever found a fix to get the engines online again? All other crews that survived the attacks, few as they were, had to be hauled to a space dock by rescuers. You're brilliant, Mari."

The compliment made her smile but it faded fast. "Brilliant would have been if I'd found a solution that didn't electrocute me," she replied honestly.

"You got our engines going and saved *The Vorge* from being boarded. Harver wouldn't have sacrificed himself for the crew. *You* did. Cathian is never going to fire you, Mari. Stop trying to impress him all the time. You don't have to work this hard."

"I'll try, but it's ingrained in me after all the years with the Teki."

"You're no longer a slave."

"I know that in my head, but this job keeps me safe. Protected. That's everything in space. Humans are captured and sold. My own parents sold me because I was worth a lot of money."

"Do you know what happened to them?"

She shook her head. "No. I never saw them again."

"Do you want me to try to find out?"

She thought about it but shook her head. "No. I cried for a long time in my bunk every night, hoping they'd come back to say they'd made a mistake by selling me. I eventually realized they wouldn't have done that to me if they really cared. I had lots of time to think about it. I never want to see them again. Nor do I want to know if they are alive or not."

Dovis nodded. "I understand. We have that in common. My parents fled our village after leaving me to die. I never sought them out or questioned what happened to them."

"Sometimes I wonder if my parents had more children. Do you ever think about that? If you have siblings?"

He shook his head. "Any siblings I have would likely shun me. Or if they were also born in skin, I doubt that they were as fortunate as I was to find someone like Taznia. It would only anger me to learn my parents had killed other children."

"You can't know that for sure. You know, about the shunning part. Maybe they aren't like your parents. I try to be fair. I'm sure there are humans out there who would never sell their children. I can't see Nara doing that. I sure wouldn't."

"The only Amarai to show me care was an elderly female who had no one else. She often told me how lonely she'd been before the day of my birth."

"I'm glad she saved you."

"I am as well."

She nodded. "I guess I should leave." She bent to pick up her toolbox.

"Don't go…"

She straightened, staring at him warily.

Dovis approached her slowly. "Are you angry with me? Feel as if I took advantage of your attraction to me?"

"No. Of course not."

He stopped advancing. "You're drawn to me against your will by chemicals in my DNA. I can't allow the medical android to run too many tests. If word reached Amarai that I had bitten you, they'd hire bounty hunters to kill me, at the very least."

"I understand. I mean, not about why they'd want to kill you. That you need to keep it secret. I only wish that you'd stop avoiding me. I don't know why you're doing so."

"To prevent us from ending up in your bed again."

That hurt. "Oh. Was it so terrible for you? Do you think I'm ugly? Teki think the appearance of humans is hideous."

"No! You are beautiful, Mari."

Her breath froze in her chest for a few heartbeats. "You really think so?"

"I know so. I find it difficult not to touch you. I always feel the urge when you're close."

She smiled, happy to hear him say those words. "Thank you. I think you're attractive, too."

He snorted. "Even like this?"

She nodded.

"I'd hurt you if I were to touch you in this form."

"Are you certain?"

She felt a surge of bravery and walked closer. He held his ground, not backing away. She reached up and placed her hands on his chest when she stopped right in front of him. The teeth *were* a bit scary. There were two sides to Dovis, though. He was still the same man who'd kissed and touched her. Slept in her bed.

"Please don't, Mari. You should never touch me when I'm in fur. You're too tempting to me."

Instead, she slid her hand up his chest, and then reached out and gently stroked the side of his face. The fur was thick and soft. His muzzle lowered, making it easier for her to stare deeply into his black eyes. His scent did such wonderful things to her body. It might be from his bite, but she didn't care. Memories of what he'd done to her were fresh in her mind; she'd dreamed about him since.

"I'm not afraid of you hurting me."

"You should be."

"I'm going to kiss you." She went up on her tiptoes, trying to reach him. It might be awkward, and she wasn't sure how his snout and her lips would meld together, but she was willing to try.

He turned his head away, grabbing her hips with his hands, and she felt the tips of his claws digging into her clothing. There was no pain, though. He lifted her and spun, striding a few steps before dropping her back on her feet. He released her fast, twisted her around, and bent her over one of the consoles. The flat, table-like surface just reached her belly.

She gasped when he pinned her there, his bigger body pressing up tight against her back. He lowered his snout, sniffing her neck…and then his fangs brushed her skin. A low growl sounded.

Her body went crazy. Her nipples beaded, her stomach had butterfly sensations buzzing throughout, and the throbbing between her legs was stronger than ever.

Dovis adjusted his hold, his claws lightly raking down her sides to her pants. He didn't hurt her, his touch gentle.

"Fuck, Mari! You should have run while you had the chance."

He reached up, tore her shirt at the shoulder, and bit her.

A jolt of pain spiked for a split second—then it became pure pleasure. She moaned, bracing her arms on the console. Heat blasted through her, as if she had a sudden and high fever. Her body reacted even stronger, until she whimpered from need. She shoved her ass back against him.

Dovis tore down her pants, hooking them with his claws to do so. He didn't cut her skin, the sharp tips feeling more like a caress. He kept his fangs locked in her shoulder, backed up his lower body for a second, but then pushed against her to pin her in place once more. His boot slid between her feet and bumped her ankle. She understood, spreading her legs farther apart.

He wrapped one of his arms around her waist, hoisted her higher, until she half lay on top of the surface in front of her. Her feet no longer touched the floor and Dovis was bent over her, keeping her from sliding off.

She was wet and aching. Dovis seemed to know, because a second later his thick shaft pushed against her now bared sex, and she cried out as he drove inside her. His cock was hard and hot. She nearly came when he was fully inside. It felt that good.

He began to thrust fast, fucking her fiercely.

Dovis made her feel things she never had before. He pounded against her ass and snarled, his fangs still locked in her shoulder. A blinding flash of ecstasy exploded through her body and Mari screamed his name.

He released her shoulder, threw back his head, and howled.

She felt his hips jerk, his cock pumping into her as more heat filled her. It sent another shockwave of pleasure through her limbs and she collapsed, panting, trying to catch her breath. She nearly blacked out from sheer bliss.

"Fuck…" Dovis stilled. Then he licked her shoulder. "Damn it." His body eased off hers and he withdrew his cock. "Did I hurt you?"

She smiled, not having the strength to even raise her head after what she'd just experienced. The console was cold against her cheek. "No."

He helped her slide down until her feet hit the floor again, and his hands were tender as he tried to pull her to a standing position. Her knees didn't want to hold her weight. Dovis lifted her into his arms, carrying her to the nearest seat. He gently put her down, trying to pull up her torn pants at the same time.

Mari noticed he was in skin when he crouched in front of her. Concern and worry showed in his eyes as he met her gaze, then his hands were on her, pushing her shirt up to check out her stomach and hips.

"You'll have bruises."

"I'm good."

He made a low rumbling sound. "You're healing quickly. But I lost control. I shouldn't have taken you that way. I'm sorry."

She smiled, feeling fantastic. It was like the time she'd fallen off a ladder while working and the medics at the station had given her a shot for pain. It had made her lightheaded and silly. "Don't be sorry. I loved every second of what happened between us."

He leaned forward, peering deeply into her eyes. "You're drunk on me."

"It's a good thing. Please don't be sorry. Can we do that again?"

He leaned even closer, resting his forehead against hers and closing his eyes. "Don't say that, Mari."

"I'm still wet." She pointed between her legs. "Soaked."

"That's from both of us," he whispered. "You were highly aroused, and I emptied my seed inside you. I'll take you to your room and help you clean up."

Chapter Nine

Mari woke alone in her bed. She remembered Dovis carrying her to her cabin and stripping off their clothing, then showering with her. Her legs had been weak for some reason, and she'd had a hard time standing straight without his help. He'd carried her to her bed afterward, tucked her in, and lain down next to her. He'd held her to make sure she was okay until she'd fallen asleep. She was pretty sure he'd stayed the entire night.

She sat up and checked the time, cursing. Her shift had started an hour ago!

Fear hit fast over getting in trouble. She was *never* late.

Mari made a mad dash to her closet and yanked out an outfit.

Her cabin door opened and she gasped, spinning to face whoever had come in.

Dovis entered carrying a tray of food. He was back to fur. It reminded her that last night, he had stayed in skin on the walk from the bridge to her cabin when he'd brought her there. They hadn't run into anyone but they could have.

"How are you feeling, Mari?"

"I'm fine but I overslept. I'm late for work!"

"You're not. I told Cathian you're taking a day off."

She gaped at him, stunned.

"It's fine, Mari. I told you he's not going to fire you. Time off is allowed and encouraged." He walked to the coffee table to put the tray down. "Come eat. How are you feeling?"

"You already asked me that, and my answer was honest."

"I'm just worried. I was rough with you." His gaze ran down her body as he approached her. "No bruises. Turn around."

She hesitated but then did as he asked. Her cheeks felt warm with her standing there totally bare to his gaze. Not even the Teki had wanted to see her that way. She looked over her shoulder at him, watching him inspect her.

"Good. You had some red marks here from my claws." His furry knuckle brushed her hip. "They're gone. Turn back around."

She did.

He moved her long hair, inspecting where he'd bitten her. "All healed and no scar." He backed up a foot. "I ordered a replacement for the pants I ruined. The Pods should deliver them outside your cabin soon. Eat. Take today off…then avoid me from now on, Mari. It's for the best. I'll deal with Raff to make sure he doesn't set us up to be alone again. Trust the computer to let you know when there's a repair to be made, not him."

Then he turned away, walking toward the door.

Hurt filled her. "That's it? We're going to pretend it didn't happen again?"

He halted but kept his back to her. "I could have hurt you, Mari. Hell, I probably did but you were too drugged on whatever my bite does to feel anything but pleasure. I'm just grateful you have no lasting injuries."

"You risked running into the crew when you carried me back to my cabin. You stayed in skin."

He remained quiet.

"Is the idea of being with me that bad? Is it because I was a slave? Because I'm human? What?"

He slowly turned, his eyes black and intense. "Ones like me don't take mates. We're not even supposed to survive into adulthood. Nothing about this is fair to you, Mari. I feel as if I'm forcing you to be with me. I kept my teeth locked inside your shoulder while I fucked you, knowing it would make you surrender to my lust. And you did. I'm an asshole."

She replayed his words, trying to make sense of them. "I'm not complaining."

"You should be! Be angry, Mari. You deserve to feel that emotion."

She walked to him. He backed up but didn't have far to go before he hit a wall.

She jabbed her finger on his chest. "Don't tell me what to feel or think, Dovis!"

His eyes widened in surprise.

"You're confusing me with this hot-and-cold routine you're doing. Like acting as if you regret what happened on the bridge last night, but then bringing me breakfast. Do you want me or not?"

He took a long time to answer. "I *do* want you, Mari. I'm just not certain if you really want *me* or if it's because I've bitten you. What if it wears out of your system completely and you end up hating me? Regretting every time I've touched you?"

She thought about that. "You left me alone for two weeks, and do you want to know what happened?"

"What?"

"I missed you. I thought about you the entire time. I kept hoping I'd run into you while I was working on repairs around *The Vorge*. Then I felt disappointed when I didn't. It wasn't because I got too close to you and your scent made me hot. And it wasn't because your DNA was still inside me. The captain had me tested a week ago, and there were no traces found. I felt that way on my own."

He appeared startled by her confession.

"I don't know anything about relationships or men, males...whatever. You're my first. I *do* know that even without you close to make my body go crazy over your scent, I wished you were. Close, that is. I understand that when you bit me, your DNA got inside me...but it's a part of you. Who you are. *What* you are."

"What are you saying?"

She thought she'd been clear, and her frustration rose. "Stop apologizing and avoiding me! I *want* this, whatever it is. I'm fine with the effect your bite has on me. More than. It feels wonderful and incredible when we're together."

He looked even more shocked, his mouth gaping open.

"I don't remember Earth. My youngest memories were living on a large transport vessel with my parents and bunch of other aliens. Then I was sold to the Teki. All kinds of aliens came to have their ships repaired. Different is my normal, Dovis. Do you understand? You warned me what to expect, told me why I felt the way I did, and I accepted that. I still do.

I'd like to get to know you and spend time with you. Even if we never feel anything deeper, and just end up having sex some more. That's not a bad thing. It's wonderful when you touch me."

"You don't mean that."

"I do. Right now, I'm aching for you. I know it's because we're this close and I can smell you. It's a physical reaction to whatever your bite does…but watch this." She spun away, stormed across the room to the farthest part of her cabin, and faced him. Long minutes passed. "I can't smell you from over here. Guess what? I still want you to stay. Would it be so bad if you stopped putting space between us and we just let this be whatever it is?"

"I could mate you by accident if I keep biting you. Mari. I'm not like other Amarai. I'm not sure what will happen. You'd be stuck with me for the rest of your life."

"Is that supposed to frighten me? It doesn't."

"It should!"

"Would you hate the idea of becoming my mate?"

"No. And that's *why* you should want me far away from you."

She shook her head. "It doesn't scare me, and I'm not asking you to leave. Look at what you did last night."

"I attacked you on the bridge."

"We had incredible sex, and then you carried me to my cabin, gently washed me, and took care of me while I recovered. This morning, you gave me the day off and even brought me breakfast. That's amazing. No one has ever been this good to me."

"You have no expectations."

"I know what I like, Dovis. That's you."

He pushed off from the wall. "Damn it, Mari! Don't tempt me. You should put some clothes on."

"Why? I'd like it better if you took off yours."

Long minutes passed...before he sighed, slowly reaching for his shirt. "I can't resist you. Please don't regret this."

"I won't."

He tore off his shirt, revealing lots of skin and muscles. "Eat first. I insist."

"Will you share it with me?"

"I already ate."

"Okay." She knew about compromising. She took a seat on the floor next to the table and dug into the food. Dovis stripped off his clothes and walked to her bed, climbing in. She was relieved. He was staying...for now.

"We should sleep in my cabin tonight, though. I have a bigger bed."

She grinned. "That's fine with me. I'm glad you're planning on letting me sleep with you. I liked it."

"Me too." He paused. "This is insane, Mari. You know that, right? We're too different."

She got up, not hungry anymore, and crossed to the bed. He looked so incredibly sexy in skin. She silently admitted she liked him better that way, as far as snuggling went. Lips meant she could kiss him. And she did just that as she curled up beside him, her mouth going to his.

He didn't hesitate to roll, pinning her under him and taking over. She moaned against his tongue.

He broke the kiss, going for her neck. "I won't bite you. I won't risk getting you with my claws or fangs."

"Whatever makes you feel more comfortable."

He chuckled and lifted his head, peering at her. "Be honest. Didn't it bother you that I bent you over and took you in fur?"

"No."

He adjusted his body, his stiff cock brushing against her. "I don't deserve you, Mari."

"Stop talking if you're only going to say negative things about us being together."

He kissed her again, and she inhaled his scent, loving the way her body couldn't seem to get enough of him. He might see it as a bad thing, but she'd never felt so alive in her life. Before, she'd just existed and survived.

Dovis was quickly becoming everything wonderful and right to her. The how or why didn't matter. His biology or whatever it was called was something she felt thankful for.

She spread her legs and wiggled until he moved on top of her. It felt natural to wrap her legs and arms around his strong body. It felt perfect when he drove his shaft into her body. They were amazing together.

*****

Dovis climbed out of bed and left Mari sleeping. He might have given her the day off, but he had to work the sleep shift. He used her shower and shifted back to fur afterward, putting on his uniform.

He went to the bridge and nodded to York. The male stood, stretched, and gave him control of the ship. "I can't believe we're hauling pets next," York muttered.

Dovis agreed. "That mission will suck."

"It has to beat some of the other things we've had to do for the Tryleskians."

"True enough."

York went to leave…then paused, staring at him with a frown.

"What?"

"You look more relaxed and less grouchy than normal. What's up with that?"

Dovis hesitated, not sure if he should answer.

"Did you sneak off to the station without me? The brothel had some nice workers. I was able to get laid. They had a Parri there." He grinned. "She was older but it didn't matter. She tied me down and had her way with me."

That surprised Dovis. "She tied you down?"

York nodded. "Parri females are into dominance over males at all times."

"I didn't know that."

"I used to hate it but after spending a few years on *The Vorge*, it was kind of nice. They like to have control. I just had to lie there and stay hard for her. Easy to do since it'd been too long since I've gotten laid."

"I'm glad for you."

York cocked his head, studying him again.

Dovis sighed and knew his friend wasn't going to leave. "Mari and I—" he began.

"What?!" York's mouth fell open and his eyes widened.

"Don't shout."

"You and Mari hooked up? She's human. And a tiny little thing. What the hell?"

"It just happened. We're together now."

York came closer. "Details, man," he demanded. "Spill them all. How? When? Why? I've heard you bitch a hundred times about Cathian being crazy for life-locking to a human. You think they're all too weak and soft. I think Mari is hot, but hell, she's too small. I would hurt her." He glanced down Dovis. "How does that even work, man? Can you kiss her with that mug of yours?"

Dovis sighed. "Don't make me regret telling you. I'm not sharing the details of my relationship with Mari. I'm just letting you know not to approach her for sex or I'll beat the hell out of you. I also didn't want you to act weird when you see us together. You tend to make a big deal out of things and get all loud."

"Does Cathian know?"

He shook his head. "Not yet. I haven't seen him."

York grinned. "You and little Mari. I never would have guessed that was possible." He suddenly sobered. "How did you even do it? She's so shy."

"I told you, I'm not answering your questions. I just wanted to inform you since you mentioned an interest in her when she first joined the crew. Keep your lips to yourself, York. She's mine."

His friend nodded. "Is this a hookup or are you claiming her?"

Dovis hesitated.

"Aw, man. You're going to break her heart, aren't you? I don't think Mari is into casual sex."

He sighed. "We're working on it. I'd like to mate her."

York grinned again and opened his mouth.

Dovis cut him off before he could speak. "Don't taunt me."

"I wasn't going to. I'm happy for you both." His expression fell though. "Shit. That means two of my friends are taken. Who's going to visit brothels with me now?"

"Raff?"

York shuddered. "No."

The bridge doors opened and Cathian walked in. "I just wanted to check on you, Dovis. You sounded off on comms when we spoke last."

"He and Mari are together," York blurted. "As in, getting undressed together and stuff."

Cathian's mouth fell open as he gawked at Dovis. "Is this true?"

He growled low, glaring at York. "*I* wanted to be the one to tell him."

"York, get out. Don't gossip with the crew," Cathian snapped. "That's an order."

York quickly fled the bridge.

Cathian walked closer, frowning. "What's going on?"

"York just told you. Mari and I are together as a couple."

"I thought you were going to avoid each other? Her attraction to you would have faded."

"It's a long story."

"I have time. Nara will understand why I'm not returning to our cabin right away."

Dovis growled low again. Cathian would want to know every detail, and he'd likely be worried he was taking advantage of Mari. And he understood that. He'd felt the same way until she'd argued with him.

"I have feelings for her…and she's aware of everything."

Cathian cocked one eyebrow.

"*Everything.*" Dovis withdrew his fur to skin. "She's seen both sides of me. I told her all about my past. I even informed her it's possible to mate her by accident with my bite. She's willing to take the risk."

He paused, waiting for his best friend to explode in anger.

Cathian surprised him by grinning. "Good. I like Mari. Treat her right."

"That's all you've got to say?"

"I want you to be happy, Dovis. Mari would make a good mate. She's loyal and sweet. It also means I won't have to buy a shock collar and have Raff help me take you down to put it on you. Mari will have you by the shaft if she's your mate." He laughed. "You won't want to frighten her off, either. Every protective instinct inside you will make damn certain of that."

Dovis stood. "We're not mated yet."

"I'm glad that you're with her." Cathian came to him, gripped his shoulders with both hands, and gave them a squeeze. "You've been alone for too long."

"I'm terrified she'll regret this one day," he admitted.

"You said you told her everything."

"I did. She argued with me for trying to avoid her. That's not what she wants. It's not what I want, either. For the first time in my life, I have hope that I'll have a mate."

Cathian nodded. "Nara has changed my life in so many wonderful ways. You could have that with Mari. She needs you as much as you do her."

He thought about that, and relaxed even more. "I already know I'd die to protect her and keep her safe."

"Exactly."

Dovis grinned. "I'm going for it. All in."

"Good."

"It's going to mean changes, though."

"Of course it will. You'll have a mate."

"That's not what I mean." Dovis took a deep breath and blew it out. "I'm going to need your support now more than I ever have."

"I'm here for you in any way you need. Always."

Chapter Ten

Mari finished her shift and placed her toolbox in the maintenance locker. It had been nice to have a day off to spend with Dovis. He'd had to work last night but he'd commed her that morning to say he'd see her after her shift, when he woke. All day while she'd worked, she imagined him in his cabin sleeping. They worked opposite hours, but it was fine. They'd work it out.

He was going to give their relationship a chance. That was all that mattered. That morning over comms, he'd even stated that intention again.

She closed the locker and turned, a smile instantly coming to her lips when she saw Dovis standing there.

"Hi! You're awake."

"I didn't sleep."

She approached him. "Are you okay?" Her stomach clenched. Had he changed his mind? Would he tell her they needed to avoid each other again? The thought made her feel physically sick.

His black eyes didn't show much emotion. Nor did his furry face. "I was thinking today."

"No." She stopped in front of him. "You said we could be together. I'm not letting you do this. We talked. Agreed! We're going to give us a chance."

He reached out and gently gripped her arms. "I want you to be my mate."

The anger and dread disappeared, replaced with surprise. That's not what she'd expected him to say.

"No uncertainty. I want you to become my mate. I think biting you may do it, but if not, I'll be going into heat in a few months. Maybe that will help. There's a lot I don't know about myself since I'm different from others of my race. We'll figure out together how to secure our mating bond to join physically for life. If you're willing… Are you, Mari?"

"Yes!" She didn't have to think about it. He was offering her a lifetime commitment. She'd be his. He'd be hers. Tears filled her eyes and she had to blink them back.

"Are you certain? I know this is fast so I need you to be sure. I couldn't take it if you agreed and then later changed your mind."

"I've never been surer, Dovis. Everything about you is wonderful to me. I don't want to lose you."

"Good." He grinned. "We'll work out the physical part of linking over time, but you *are* my mate from this moment forward. Agreed?"

"Yes! I'm yours. You're mine."

"Thank God…because today while you were working, I packed up your few possessions. I want you to live with me. I added you to the access for the lock on my cabin. It's now yours, too."

"Okay." The idea of sleeping with him every night—well, when he wasn't on shift—made her overjoyed. They'd work everything else out. That's what couples did. The most important part was, they'd be together. No worries of losing him, or him walking away. Mates were for life.

He began to shapeshift. His fur receded, along with his snout. His claws against her became just firm fingers. He smiled at her when he was done and leaned forward, brushing his lips against hers. She threw her arms around his neck and deepened the kiss.

He growled and broke away, breathing hard. "Stop, or I'll take you right here."

"Do it. I want you," she breathed, throbbing in all the right places.

He chuckled. "Always encouraging me, Mari. We need to inform the crew we're mates."

"Now?"

"Yes. I called a meeting in the dining room that starts in ten minutes. I want to tell all of them at the same time that you're mine."

She was a bit blown away. "You've gone from hot and cold, to one-hundred percent committed. May I ask why? Not that I'm complaining. I'm not, by any means. Just curious, now that the shock is wearing off."

"I thought about what life would be like both with and without you today. That's why I didn't sleep. I decided I want everything with you, Mari. *Everything.* I don't know if we can breed children together but I hope we can. Hell, I hope they're different like I am, if they're born looking Amarain. I've been ashamed of what I am for my entire life...but this ability to shapeshift is what made it possible to be your mate. I like kissing you with my lips and not having to worry about my claws cutting your skin in this form while I make love to you." He reached up and caressed her cheek with his fingertip. "But I can defend and protect you better in fur. Now both sides of me belong to you. That's my vow. You're my mate."

She was his mate. That kept circling in her mind and happiness burst inside her. "I love you, Dovis. I want you to know that. My entire life, all I've wanted was someone who cared about me...but you're more. You're everything I never dreamed I'd find. I'd do anything for you."

"Mari..." he leaned close and kissed her, a light brush of his lips over hers. He backed up and smiled. "You're my heart. Let's go inform the crew. I want everyone to know you're mine."

She nodded, blinking back more tears. "Do you think they'll take it well?"

"Yes. I have to admit, I already told York and Cathian we were together. Just not that we were mates. They were both supportive. Everyone will be. No worries, Mari."

"Good."

He released her and offered his arm. She took it, and he led her toward the lift. They waited for it, and once inside, Mari stared up at him expectantly when the doors closed, taking them to the dining room level.

"What?"

"You're still in skin."

He smiled. "I know."

"I don't understand..."

"You will." He winked. "Trust me?"

"Of course. You're my mate."

"I love hearing you say that."

The doors opened, and he led her out, keeping a firm hold on her arm. She followed him, feeling a bit worried. He still didn't shift back to fur, not even when the auto doors to the dining area of the ship opened. He kept walking forward until they stopped feet inside.

The entire crew were assembled at various tables. Raff sat alone on one side. Midgel on the other. The Pods sat with Captain Cathian and Nara. Marrow sat at a table with York. All of them had drinks.

Everyone turned their way.

York dropped his drink and was on his feet in a heartbeat, snarling and flashing fangs. "Who the fuck are you?" He reached for the weapon strapped on his hip. "Get the hell away from her!"

Midgel gasped and slid off her chair, slipping under the table to hide.

Marrow's chair crashed to the floor as she moved to stand beside York, lifting her fists and readying her body in a fighting stance.

Raff took a sip of his drink and smirked. He didn't say a word.

The Pods just stared at them from their chairs but they were looking at Dovis with open curiosity. None of them showed fear.

Cathian grabbed Nara and pulled her onto his lap when she tried to get out of the way in case a fight broke out. He grinned, staring at Mari and Dovis. "Good to *see* you, my friend."

"You know this asshole?" York kept his hand on his weapon. "Who is he, Captain? Did he slip aboard when we were at Grover station? Hey, asshole, *let Mari go*. My friend will rip your pretty face off if he sees you standing that close to her. He's not one to piss off."

Dovis chuckled. "Pretty? You think I have a pretty face?" He glanced at Mari. "Do I?"

"Handsome," she corrected.

"What the fuck?" York muttered. "You dumped Dovis for this jerk? Come on, Mari. Dovis is way better than this...*whatever* he is." He leaned toward Marrow, muttering, "What the hell is he? Do you know his race?"

"Never seen one quite like him before," she responded.

Raff stood.

"Now you're in for it, invader. He's an assassin," York taunted. "He knows a thousand ways to kill your ass."

Raff walked over to refill his drink and chuckled. "This is funnier than shit. They have no clue. Midgel, get off the floor. You're safe." Raff crossed the room and retook his seat.

"What in the *hell* is going on?" York shot a glare at Raff. "Do you know this alien?"

Cathian continued to smile. "We *all* know him. Stand down, York. Marrow. It's fine."

"I don't know him," Nara whispered.

Cathian kissed the top of her head and kept hold of her on his lap. "Yes, you do."

Mari was amused. She wondered if they'd figure it out on their own. The Pods kept quiet. They clearly knew, but seemed too busy staring at Dovis to say anything. She was pretty sure they might have already known he was a shapeshifter, but this was the first time they'd seen him without fur.

Dovis finally spoke again. "Sit your big blue ass down, York. You still pondering which mouth of a Teki to kiss?"

York's mouth fell open and his eyes widened. "How did you…" He paused, frowning, studying Dovis.

"I know you called dibs on Mari." Dovis shook his head. "You will never have her. She's mine."

York stumbled back, hit a table, and his ass sank to the surface. "*Dovis?* What the fuck, man? Is that you?"

Marrow swayed on her feet a little, paling. "*What?* That can't be him."

Dovis looked at her. "I never would have punched you in the arm if hadn't kept trying to grab my dick. Now I expect you to *never* try it again." He glanced around. "I wanted everyone to know that Mari has agreed to be my mate. I figured I'd tell you in this form rather than my other one, to avoid some awkward questions about our sex life."

Marrow just sank to her knees on the floor, gaping at Dovis. "No way! Shapeshifter? How the fuck did we not know?"

Midgel climbed out from under the table and retook her seat. She crossed her arms and her whiskers twitched, but she said nothing.

"We always wondered about your appearance," One stated. "We weren't sure what Mari's idea of attractive was until now. She thought it a lot though when you revealed this side of you to her. She likes to kiss that mouth a lot."

"Congratulations on mating," Three said. "Mari is certain."

"Stop second-guessing her, Dovis," Two added. "She won't change her mind."

"How the fuck?" York got back to his feet and crossed the room, stopping right in front of Dovis. "It's *really* you? You're a shapeshifter?"

"Yes. It's always been a secret but...you're my crew. My family."

York reached out his hands and gently gripped Dovis by the face, leaning in to get a better look.

"Don't kiss him," Raff called out. "He'll grow that snout right out in about three seconds flat and make you regret it."

York let him go and glanced back. "I wasn't going to kiss him, jerk. I'm just in shock." He stared at Dovis. "Fuck. You're *pretty*, man! Why didn't you tell me?"

"It's a long story but I plan to share it with you. We'll sit down with drinks."

"We've got plenty of them here," Cathian reminded them. "Come on. Everyone sit down. I'm so happy for you both. To Mari and Dovis being mates! Midgel, serve the happy couple please."

"I'm on it." Midgel rushed to do his bidding.

Dovis felt everything had gone better than expected when he revealed the truth to his crew. He led Mari to the table where their captain sat and helped her take a seat before he sat next to her. He took her hand and lifted it to his lips, kissing the back. She grinned, appearing happy. He could relate.

"He really *is* a werewolf," Nara muttered. "They exist! I learn something new in space all the time."

Mari glanced at her. "What's a werewolf?"

Nara pointed at Dovis. "*Him*. It's a scary-ass wolf that can turn into a hot guy." She smiled then. "That's so awesome that you two are mated. That means we get to keep you forever, since Dovis and Cathian are best friends."

Dovis leaned in to Mari. "She's mine, and *I* get to keep her forever."

His mate reached up to caress his face. "Forever sounds perfect."

He loved her touch and staring into her eyes. He had such a beautiful mate. She was the most wonderful thing that had ever happened to him. He glanced around at his crew. They were his family.

His life had once been filled with loneliness but not anymore. All the anger and resentment he'd harbored since childhood faded from his soul. Mari and his family healed those wounds in his heart.

Love could do that.

Not the end. Up next...York's story.

About the Author

NY Times and USA Today Bestselling Author

I'm a full-time wife, mother, and author. I've been lucky enough to have spent over two decades with the love of my life and look forward to many, many more years with Mr. Laurann. I'm addicted to iced coffee, the occasional candy bar (or two), and trying to get at least five hours of sleep at night.

I love to write all kinds of stories. I think the best part about writing is the fact that real life is always uncertain, always tossing things at us that we have no control over, but when writing you can make sure there's always a happy ending. I love that about being an author. My favorite part is when I sit down at my computer desk, put on my headphones to listen to loud music to block out everything around me, so I can create worlds in front of me.

For the most up to date information, please visit my website. www.LaurannDohner.com

Printed in Great Britain
by Amazon